THE SIXTH SENSE
SECRETS FROM BEYOND
RUNAWAY

2

By David Benjamin

SCHOLASTIC INC.
New York   Toronto   London   Auckland   Sydney
Mexico City   New Delhi   Hong Kong

ISBN 0-439-20271-X

12 11 10 9 8 7 6 5 4 3 2 1   0 1 2 3 4 5 6/0

Printed in the U.S.A.

First Scholastic printing, November 2000

ONE

Scared. Cole Sear was used to waking up scared. He was used to being jolted from sleep, torn from the safety of his dreams.

This time was different.

He opened his eyes into the darkness. At first he didn't know where he was. This wasn't the darkness of his room, or his house. He rolled over and felt the floor beneath his sleeping bag. Now he knew where he was. His friend Jason's room, in his friend Jason's house.

Safe.

Cole heard footsteps in the house. Shuffling at first, careful. A door opening then closing. More footsteps. Going from room to room now.

Cole sat up and looked at the clock.

5 A.M.

He heard the voices of Jason's parents. Whispering loudly, starting to argue. He saw the hall light turn on, then heard them coming to the door. He closed his eyes and pretended to sleep. He didn't want them to think he was awake.

"Jason?"

Mrs. Black's voice was gentle, but Cole could recognize the fear beneath.

Cole opened his eyes. Jason was still sound asleep — safe, but only for a moment longer.

"*Jason.*" Mr. Black's voice had a harder edge.

Jason stirred and pulled the bed sheet over his head. "What?" he mumbled.

"Do you know where Ted is?"

Ted was Jason's older brother. Cole had only met him once before. He seemed cool, but he was never really around. He was sixteen years old and didn't feel the need to talk to his eleven-year-old brother's friends.

"How should I know?" Jason groaned. "What time is it?"

"It's late," Mrs. Black said. "Very late. Ted isn't home yet and some of his things are gone. Did he tell you where he was going?"

Jason shook his head, awake now. "Didn't he leave a note?" he asked.

"He didn't leave a note or a message on the answering machine."

"Maybe you just didn't find it," Jason said. "Let me look."

He pushed himself out of bed and stumbled past his parents. For the first time since they'd come to the room, Mr. and Mrs. Black noticed Cole lying on the floor.

"Sorry to wake you," Mrs. Black said, trying to muster up some kindness. But mostly she sounded sad and worried.

Cole stayed in Jason's room as the Blacks searched the house. He felt strange being here, especially when something was so clearly wrong. Even though Jason was the closest thing he had to a best friend, there was still a lot they didn't know about each other. And Cole was pretty sure that Jason wouldn't want him around if his family was having problems. Cole knew how that felt. For a long time, he'd never invite friends over to his house. First it was because his parents were arguing. Then it was because his father had left. Finally it was for other reasons — reasons much harder to explain, even to friends.

Cole could hear the Blacks calling out to one another, finding basketball tickets and movie stubs and scribbled notes that had nothing to do with where Ted was. After a few minutes, Jason's mom sounded really upset.

"He's gone," she started to insist, over and over again. "I'm telling you, he's gone."

Mr. Black told her to stop saying such things.

Jason remained quiet. Searching.

A bicycle chain rattled outside, and Cole glanced out the open window.

The biker wasn't Ted at all, just an older man collecting cans from the trash. As a gust of wind blew from the street, Cole shivered. He turned back to the room, catching a glimpse of something on Jason's desk. Among a sea of papers, pencils, and gum wrappers, a neatly folded sheet of notebook paper was sticking up from between the keys of Jason's computer.

On it were two words:

TO JASON

Cole and Jason had been using the computer before they went to sleep.

The note hadn't been there.

Suddenly Cole felt cold. Bone cold.

As he grabbed the note, he shook. He tried to ignore the cold, but it wouldn't let him go. The cold was at the heart of his deepest secret. The cold could only mean one thing.

When the dead people come, you feel cold. You see your breath, and you know they are near.

"Jason!" he called out, pressing the note in his hand.

The word left his mouth in a small, wispy cloud of frozen air.

Cole felt the hairs on the back of his neck rise. Somebody was behind him. *Close* behind him. He was afraid to turn. He looked into the window and saw the reflection.

It wasn't Jason.

It was someone worse.

Someone dead.

TWO

Cole didn't move. He just watched as the figure moved closer in the reflection. He would not let the man know he was paying attention. He would stay still and hope the dead man would go away.

He should have been used to this by now, but he wasn't.

Would he ever be?

"It's all my fault," the man moaned.

Instantly Cole knew who it was. Not his name or where he came from. Just his mangled appearance and his death-knell voice. His eyes, red and glassy, glared from a face blackened by flames. Thin, burned clumps of reddish-gray hair hung limply from the right side of his head, thinning out to a black bubble of skin where the left side of his face used to be. His left ear was gone.

"I hurt them all."

The man had died in a plane crash. Then he had found Cole.

Now he wouldn't let go.

Cole had tried to talk to him. Sometimes that's what the dead people wanted — someone to listen to them and help them fix their problems so they could move on. But talking hadn't worked with this one. He followed Cole everywhere. And now he was here, in Jason's house, with Jason's frantic family in the next room. *They* wouldn't be able to see the dead man, but Cole definitely could. He could see him, hear him, and feel his cold presence.

Still, he would not turn around.

He knew the man's face would be twisted in pathetic agony, but no tears would come. He'd seen it many times before.

"CAN'T YOU UNDERSTAND — I HURT THEM ALL!"

Cole closed his eyes. He tried to ignore the yelling and the chill. He heard Jason calling him from what seemed like a mile away.

"What is it, Cole?"

Cole opened his eyes and saw Jason peering at him from the doorway.

The dead man was gone.

"What?" Cole said, a little too loudly.

"You called me, I thought." Jason looked confused and concerned. "Didn't you?"

Cole remembered the note crumpled in his hand. He tried to keep his hand steady as he handed it over.

"I found this on your keyboard," he explained.

Jason recognized the handwriting. He'd just woken up, but now he looked like he hadn't slept in days.

"Mom . . . Dad?" Jason called out.

Mr. and Mrs. Black rushed in and Jason unfolded the note. Standing at his side, Cole could read it clearly.

J,

Now listen don't freak out OK, I AM COMING BACK, just not 4 awhile. i don't know how long. I cant tell U where i'm going cause I don't know and thats the truth. I just have to get out and do some things. IT'S NOT BECAUSE OF YOU ok? it's not because of any 1 really except me, well, mom and dad too. I just can't stand being in this house any more J, too much PRESSURE around here.

*You will understand some day when U R older
I promise. in the meantime just remember
don't be like me and whatever U do, DON'T
TELL M&D ABOUT THIS NOTE! Just tell
them you heard from a friend that I'm ok &
I will be back when things R better.*

B good,

yr bro, Ted

"Oh, please no," Mrs. Black cried.

"I'm making some phone calls right now — I don't care who I wake up," Mr. Black said, storming out of the room. Mrs. Black followed.

Jason still held the note. He was reading it and rereading it, as if he could rearrange the words on the page and find where Ted had gone. Cole didn't know what to do. He wanted to ask Jason if he was okay — but that was a really stupid question.

Jason was clearly not okay.

Cole thought that maybe Jason had forgotten he was there. But then his friend looked up at him and said, "Ted's threatened to run away before. He's never actually done it."

As if he owed Cole an explanation.

"Do you want me to go home?" Cole asked quietly.

Jason looked at him blankly.

"No. You didn't see Ted come in and leave the note, did you?"

Cole shook his head. He had actually slept well, for the first time in a while.

"Neither did I," Jason said sadly.

Cole could hear all the *if only*s caught in Jason's head. *If only I'd been able to stop him. If only I'd been awake, I could have yelled at him not to leave.*

Cole knew what it was like to live with *if only*s. For more than a year after his father left, *if only*s were all he could feel. *If only I had been a better son. If only I had been able to stop Mom and Dad from fighting. If only he had seen how much we needed him.*

If only I had had a chance to say good-bye.

Cole could hear Mr. and Mrs. Black in the next room, making phone calls across the pre-dawn city, hoping to find Ted.

"Charlie? It's Pete Black. Listen, I'm sorry to wake you, but Ted didn't come home tonight and I wonder if Kent knows where he is. . . ."

But Kent didn't know. Neither did Jackson or Joanie or Madalina.

Mr. Black was shouting on the phone now, calling all the phone numbers on Ted's phone list. He wasn't shouting out of meanness — only desperation. Mrs. Black told him to calm down a little, but he shrugged her off. She came into Jason's room with a cordless phone and held out her hand to Jason. He gave her the note.

"I'm sorry about this," she said again, to both of them this time. Her voice was so familiar to Cole — it was the same voice his own mother used when everything was falling apart. It was like the voice of a woman who had managed to get out of a burning building, and was focusing on the one thing she'd managed to save instead of all the other things she had lost. In Cole's mom's case, Cole was the thing that remained. He prayed that the same thing wouldn't happen to Jason. He prayed that Ted would be found soon.

From the other room, Mr. Black cursed and kicked a wall. "The police have me on hold!" he yelled, storming into the hall. "My son is missing and they *put me on hold.* They say there's not much they can do until he's been missing for twenty-four hours. I keep telling them it might be too late by then, but do they care? No! I just can't get through to them."

For the first time that night, Cole felt he could do something to help. He knew someone in the Philadelphia police department who would be willing to talk to the Blacks and try to find Ted. Detective Brown had told Cole to call him at any time of the day or night if there was an emergency.

Cole figured this was an emergency now.

He quickly dug into his backpack and found Detective Brown's card.

"Call him," he told Mr. Black, handing over the number. "He'll answer. He always does."

A half hour later, Detective James Brown was striding up the front walk, briefcase in hand. He'd obviously come straight from bed. His hat was on a little crooked. His chin was unshaven. His dark skin was even darker under his eyes.

Cole was surprised by how relieved he was to see Detective Brown. Even though the detective reminded him of all these horrible things he'd been through — the aftermath of a plane crash, a number of angry dead people — the cop's presence was still reassuring. He was one of two people in the world who knew Cole's secret (Cole's mom was the other). Cole trusted Detective Brown. And in some strange way, he felt that Detective Brown trusted him, too.

"Thank you for coming at this hour," Mrs. Black greeted him. "We're sorry to wake you up on a Sunday. Is there any news?"

"I've radioed all the information you gave me to

the dispatcher," Detective Brown said as he stepped into the house, nodding a greeting to Cole and Jason. "Physical description, favorite hangouts, and so on. The surrounding precincts have all been notified and squad cars are combing the metro area as we speak. If Ted's out there, we'll find him."

"*If* —" Mrs. Black said anxiously, horrified by a single two-letter word. "You think it's possible he's *not* out there?"

"I didn't mean it that way," Detective Brown reassured her, putting a hand on her shoulder. "In most of these cases, the kids come back within twenty-four hours — or we pick them up when they try to get money or contact home. Usually they're grateful to see us, even if they don't admit it. You did the right thing by calling me — I'm glad Cole gave you my number. You can never be too cautious." He sat on the living room sofa and pulled a pen and a legal pad from his briefcase. "Now if you don't mind, I need to ask some questions."

Cole hovered on the outside of the living room as Jason and his parents talked to Detective Brown. The detective didn't pay much attention to Cole — not because he didn't care about him, but because Cole couldn't answer any of his questions about Ted Black. It was strange for Cole to be only an observer. He was used to being asked questions all the time:

What happened, Cole? What are you looking at? Why are you acting this way? Who are you talking to?

He felt he never had the right answers . . . until three people helped him. The first was a psychologist named Malcolm Crowe, who was gone now. The second was his mom. The third was Detective Brown. They helped Cole find out the truth — about the dead people, and about himself.

The truth was scary. But at least Cole knew he wasn't alone.

He could sense that Jason and his parents were feeling less alone, too, now that Detective Brown was there and vowing to make things happen. But Cole could tell there was something else that Detective Brown was holding back. Something that would make the Blacks feel even more shaken.

Detective Brown put down his pen for a moment and looked at Mr. and Mrs. Black. His glance was pointed, but his tone was muted and careful.

"Has Ted been hanging around lately with any kids from outside his usual group? Maybe from a different neighborhood or school?"

"Not that we know of," Mr. Black replied warily. "Why?"

"I don't want to alarm you, but the Philadelphia

14

police department has been looking into the disappearance of five teens in the area — good kids from good families, maybe a little rebellious and sick of living at home, but not the kind of runaway who usually goes for that long. Ted fits the profile."

"And these other five . . ." Mrs. Black began hesitantly. "You don't know where they are?"

Detective Brown shook his head. "No, but we're looking."

"Could they have been kidnapped?" Mr. Black asked. "Stolen off the street or something?"

"There's no evidence of that — no ransom notes or eyewitness reports or anything," Detective Brown answered. "We can't rule it out, but right now we're focusing on finding a common place they might have gone. Somewhere we don't know. I'm only bringing this up because the news stations are about to break the story, and I wanted you to hear it from me first. Ted might not have anything to do with the other runaways. As I said before, it's likely we'll find him in the next twenty-four hours . . . or that he'll come back home again on his own. In the meantime, we'll follow all the leads. So if you could give me any more information . . . some photos, the addresses and phone numbers of his friends, maybe a look at his computer. . . ."

As Detective Brown headed up to Ted's room with Mr. and Mrs. Black, Jason stayed in the living room with Cole.

"It's so stupid," Jason said.

"What is?" Cole asked quietly.

Jason looked at him directly, and Cole knew that his friend was glad he was there.

"If Ted were here right now, he'd see that Mom and Dad actually love him. When he's around they like to pick on him — especially Dad. Ted doesn't take it very well. Sometimes he makes it worse by yelling. But he shouldn't have done this. I'm so mad at him."

Cole didn't hear any anger in his friend's voice. Only fear.

"He's out there somewhere," Jason said, pointing to the window. Cole knew that the *out there* he meant wasn't the quiet street on the other side of the glass, where sunrise was about to break. No, *out there* was an unknown place. It could be a dark alley or a abandoned building or a train traveling far away. For Cole, *out there* was an unreachable, untouchable place. It was where his father lived with a woman who wasn't Cole's mother, in a house where Cole would never have a room.

Cole wanted to tell Jason he knew how he felt.

He knew what it was like when somebody disappeared from your life. But at the same time, he didn't want to tell Jason about it, because he couldn't give Jason the ending he needed. Cole's father never came back. Cole was still hoping that Ted would.

"I don't know if they're going to find him," Jason whispered, even though his parents were in another part of the house. "He doesn't only hang out at the mall, Cole. I mean, I told the detective where he usually went, but I don't think the police will find him there. I think some of the guys Ted was hanging out with weren't really into the police."

"Jason?" Mr. Black's voice cut through the house. "Can you come up here?"

Jason left to help his mom and dad. Cole stayed in the living room. Suddenly, he was exhausted. He closed his eyes and listened to the sounds in the house. The muted voices belonged to Detective Brown and Ted's family. The silence that crept through every room of the house belonged to Ted. His absence was the presence everyone felt.

Cole fell back asleep. He was woken up a few minutes later by Detective Brown. Jason and his parents were still upstairs.

Detective Brown hadn't meant to wake him up. But he seemed glad when Cole opened his eyes.

"How are you doing?" he asked.

"Okay," Cole said.

"You did the right thing, having them call me."

Cole nodded.

"Take care of your friend, okay? And call me if anything else comes up."

Cole nodded again.

"They're a good family, right?"

Cole shrugged. He wasn't sure what a good family was. He *thought* Jason's family was one . . . but the only thing he had to compare it to was his own.

Now it was Detective Brown's turn to nod.

"Say hi to your mom for me," he said as he headed to the door. "And don't worry — this one will have a happy ending."

Cole watched the detective leave the house, stepping into the dawn's newborn sunlight. He wished he could believe him one hundred percent. He wished he could believe that there would be a happy ending.

Cole had a sense that he'd see Ted again.

But he wasn't sure whether Ted would be alive or dead.

THREE

When Cole woke up for the third time that morning, Jason was dressed and ready to go.

"What's up?" Cole asked, wiping the sleep out of his eyes.

"Still no word from Ted," Jason replied. "Dad's out driving. Mom's staying by the phone. A few of her friends are over. It's basically chaos."

"What do you want to do?"

"I want to look for Ted."

Jason was totally serious. It only took Cole one look to know this. And it took less than a look for Cole to know that he would go along. Because Jason needed him. And Jason was his friend.

First, Cole used Mrs. Black's cell phone to call his mom. He wasn't sure what to tell her — if he mentioned Ted's disappearance, she'd be worried and might not let him stay around. But if he didn't mention that Ted was missing, she would wonder why he couldn't tell her a specific time he'd be home.

In the end, it was Jason's presence that made Cole choose what to say. With Jason right beside him, he didn't want to go into all the details. It was as if the more people you told, the more real the problem became.

Luckily, his mom had been wanting to take an extra shift at work that Sunday — there were documents that needed sorting, and she never got the peace and quiet to do it during the week. So when Cole asked if he could stay over at Jason's for the entire day, his mom was totally fine with it. He knew she was happy he had found some real friends. For a while, his life had been so crazy that friends were hard to come by. Not anymore. Not with Jason.

It was a little harder to persuade Mrs. Black to let them go. They swore they wouldn't go far. (As far as Cole knew, this was the truth.) She didn't want to let Jason out of her sight, but her friends convinced her that it wasn't right to keep Jason cooped up in the house as they waited for news about Ted. In the end, a compromise was reached — Jason and Cole would take Mrs. Black's cell phone with them, and would come back immediately if she called.

Jason and Cole headed to the back of the laundry room, where the Blacks kept their bikes. Ted's bicycle leaned upright on the wall, his helmet askew on the handlebars. Cole looked at it with a mix of awe and dread. Clearly Ted had left the house on foot . . . or had been picked up in the darkest part of the night.

Ted's bike was too big for Cole, but luckily Jason had an old bike that Cole could ride. Together they pedaled through the neighborhood, stopping off at pizza places and record stores. Jason had grabbed a picture of him and Ted, and was showing it to all the store clerks and owners. Most of them said the police had already been by, asking the same question. They all wished Jason luck . . . and said they hadn't seen Ted in the past few days or weeks.

While Jason talked to the shopkeepers, Cole studied the photo he'd brought. It couldn't be that old — Jason looked pretty much the same in the picture as he did now. They were on a family vacation, and clearly their parents had asked Ted and Jason to pose together. Ted looked happy; you couldn't tell that anything was wrong. His dark hair fell down to his shoulders and over one eye. Jason had a short cut and lighter hair . . . but still it was obvious that he and Ted were brothers. They had the same smile — a little sarcastic, not too wide.

Cole had always wondered what it would be like to have a brother or a sister. He couldn't imagine sharing his family with anyone else. But it would be cool to have someone else around, someone to help him out every now and then.

Jason was acting like he'd lost a part of himself, and now was desperately trying to get it back. But the shopkeepers couldn't help him and Cole couldn't really help him. Finally, he took a torn piece of paper out of his pocket.

"I guess we should try this," he said. Cole saw the sheet read GRENDEL'S, followed by a street address he didn't recognize.

"I heard Ted mention Grendel's on the phone once," Jason explained. "And then I found this in Ted's room, under his guitar."

"Did you tell Detective Brown?" Cole asked.

"No, this was after he left."

"We could call him."

"No. I want to check it out first."

Soon they were biking past the familiar buildings, with Jason in the lead. They were heading into a different neighborhood now — abandoned and industrial. The streets were silent but for the soft blasts of a distant riveting machine. A thin black cat bristled against an abandoned truck dock, then bolted away as soon as Jason and Cole sped near.

Cole was reminded of a game he used to play with his father. Really, it was his father's game, and Cole just played along. They would wander from street to street, with no sense of direction, no map to guide them. Mr. Sear would ask Cole a direction, and when Cole said "left," they'd go left. Or if he said "straight," they'd go straight. Cole's dad liked to point out things — strange street signs, or half-demolished buildings. To him, this was more exciting than any museum. Cole's mom said their wanderings were crazy stuff. But back then, she was smiling when she said it.

Crazy stuff was Cole's dad's specialty, as it turned out — in more ways than one. He also did things like leaving the family without warning. Like calling to say hi seven months later from his new house, where he was living with a lady who collected tolls on the expressway.

That was one of the reasons Cole no longer liked crazy stuff. Riding through a strange neighborhood like this made him nervous. But he couldn't tell Jason to turn back. He was pretty sure Jason would go on without him.

Finally they reached the address. The sign outside didn't say GRENDEL'S — instead it read JLM AUTO REPAIR above a gaping entrance. Jason and Cole locked their bikes and their helmets onto the base of a street lamp and headed toward the cavernous inside. They were stopped by a sharp-faced guy in sunglasses.

"Sorry, no visitors," he said, blocking their way.

"My brother told me to meet him here — this is Grendel's, right?" Jason said, as if he knew what was inside.

The guy at the door eased up a little.

"Who's your brother?" he asked.

"Ted Black," Jason replied, real calm.

"Never heard of him. But I'm really bad with names. Go and take a look."

With that, Jason and Cole were waved inside, through a curtain that blocked out a lot of the sun. From the outside, the building looked pretty simple. But inside it was a mess. There were guys (and some girls) scattered around — most of them teens, a couple a little younger. Nobody as young as Cole and Jason. There were a few video games against the walls and an air hockey table that whirred in anticipation of the next match. Most of the people were just hanging around — smoking and chatting and dozing on mismatched couches. A few groups hung in clusters, laughing and poking at one another over pinball machines and bags of chips. Cole could see the curtained doorway to a back room, but he couldn't make out what was going on there. Even though it was light out, it was very dark inside.

Jason and Cole moved cautiously through the arcade, staying close to each other. No one seemed to notice them, except a slouchy young guy wearing a goatee that was more shadow than actual hair. "Need change?" he asked, jiggling his hand absently in a large cup of coins.

"Okay," Cole said, digging out a dollar from his pocket.

The guy gave him a look. "Only a dollar?"

"Actually," Jason said, nervous now, "we're looking for my brother, Ted Black. Have you seen him?"

"I don't remember names," the guy said.

Suddenly, a glimpse of aqua blue caught Cole's eye. In the corner, near an old Coke machine, he saw someone Ted's height, with Ted's kind of hair.

"There!" Cole blurted out. He headed toward the Coke machine, darting through a cluster of kids that stood between them.

"Hey!" someone called out as Cole passed. But Cole wasn't paying any attention.

Still the delay had been too much. By the time Cole got to where he'd seen the figure, Ted — or the person who'd looked like him — was gone.

"What's going on?" Jason asked, coming up behind him.

"I thought I saw something," Cole explained vaguely. He didn't want to tell Jason what he'd seen unless he was sure.

Cole was about to say something else, but he was interrupted by a spiteful, snarky voice.

"Hey, little guy," the voice snarled.

Cole and Jason spun around. Three kids approached. They couldn't have been more than two or three years older than Cole and Jason, but they tried to compensate with their attitude. The one who'd called Cole "little guy" wasn't that much bigger than Cole. But he had a fire in his eyes — definite trouble.

"Yeah you, little guy," he said again. His red hair was scraggly and his skin was pale. He spread apart his arms, revealing a soaking wet T-shirt bearing the name of a rock group in letters too messed up to be readable. "You see this shirt? You did this. You knocked against me and spilled my . . . Shirley Temple."

The two sidekicks snickered.

"I'm sorry," Cole said. "I didn't mean to."

"*'I didn't mean to,'*" the ringleader mimicked in a singsong voice. "How about you give me all your quarters and we'll call it even."

Reaching shakily into his pocket, Cole pulled out the four quarters he'd just gotten, along with a nickel and three pennies. "Um, I can get more from the change guy," he offered.

"I can get some, too," Jason chimed in.

"How about we shake you upside down and see what falls out of your pocket?" one of the sidekicks said. The other two seemed to like the idea. They moved in closer.

Cole looked for a way out, but he and Jason were up against a wall. Cole was scared — he always tried to avoid fights. He didn't know *how* to fight.

These kids did.

And they were ready for a fight now.

FOUR

The snarly redhead shoved Jason. Jason shoved back harder. Then, surprising Cole, he looked over the redhead's shoulder and yelled, "Devon!"

One of the other kids lunged for Cole, but Cole dodged away. The kid stumbled against the Coke machine. Cole managed to put a table between himself and the remaining attacker. But Jason was still out there against the ringleader. As Cole watched, he aimed a punch at Jason. Jason knocked it aside and delivered his own blow.

Cole had never seen him like this before.

Suddenly, a new person had joined the fray. Roughly Ted's age, he stepped between Jason and the redhead, pushing them apart. Cole figured this was Devon, the kid Jason had called out to.

"What's up, Merv?" Devon said to the ringleader. "You starting trouble again?"

"He spilled something on me!" Merv protested. But as soon as he said it, even he seemed to know how weak he sounded.

"Let 'em go or I'll make sure they never let you in here again," Devon warned him firmly.

"Yeah, okay," Merv grumbled. He and the other two reluctantly slumped away . . . and shot Cole and Jason a set of evil, threatening looks.

"Yeah, don't try that again!" Jason said indignantly, brushing himself off. He was still hyped up from the fight. "Thanks, Devon."

"What are you doing here?" Devon replied flatly. He didn't seem happy to see Jason.

"Looking for Ted," he said. Then he turned to Cole and said, "Devon's one of Ted's best friends."

"Who sent you here, your mom and dad?" Devon snapped.

"Maybe," Jason answered. "Is he here?"

Devon rolled his eyes and started to walk back to the video games. "Maybe."

"You know something, don't you?"

"Look, I *know* that Ted doesn't need you," Devon shot back. Then, he eased up a little. "I'm sure you're worried about your brother. But you don't have to be. He can take care of himself. He's always liked you, Jason, but you just have to let him go for now. You should go home. This place is full of stupid punks like Merv, and the next time you meet one, I won't save your hide."

"The police are looking for Ted," Cole said, thinking that maybe if Devon knew this, he'd realize how serious the situation was.

But Devon wasn't impressed. "It figures," he said. "As if he's a criminal for wanting to get away."

"So you know he ran away!" Jason said.

"I didn't say that. Let's just say that I saw it coming. He felt like your parents would never respect him. He felt that maybe if he wasn't there, there wouldn't be all the constant yelling and fighting."

"It's not that bad!" Jason argued. "Tell him I said that."

"I would if I could, man. I'll be honest with you — I haven't seen your brother in a few days. He was hanging with a new crowd."

"Who?" Jason asked.

"I don't really know. I just knew he wasn't with me and the rest of his old friends. But I'll tell you what — if I see him, I'll tell him you were looking."

With that, Devon shrugged and walked away.

"Hey — wait a sec!" Jason shouted, tailing him.

Cole tried to follow, but at that second there was

a rush of people to a pinball machine where some-one was beating the high score. He looked around for an open path.

From a dark corner, he noticed someone staring at him — a tall guy in an army surplus jacket.

"Lose someone?" the guy asked.

"My friend," Cole replied. "And my friend's brother —"

"Ted, right?"

"Yeah." Cole tried to sound casual. "Do you know where he is?"

"I might." The guy was looking around — Cole couldn't tell whether he was just easily distracted, or whether he was searching out someone in partic-ular. "I'm Eddie. What's your name?"

It was a simple question to answer. But suddenly Cole's thoughts were hijacked. A familiar figure stag-gered toward him through the crowd — the man with the burned-off ear.

"Not again," Cole said under his breath.

Eddie looked puzzled. "It's the first time I asked you."

"You are looking . . . wrong place!" the man with the burned-off ear cried out, flailing his right arm. *"It's this way."*

Cole narrowed his eyes. "Which way?"

"Who are you talking to?" Eddie asked.

"Talk to her. You must talk to her. Tell her it's all my fault."

"Talk to who?" Cole asked.

"Hey, kid," Eddie snapped, "are you trying to play with my head? Because you are doing a superior job of it right now."

The man let out a garbled moan, a name Cole couldn't recognize.

"Who?" Cole called out to the man. "What did you say?"

"You heard me!" Eddie replied, getting angry now.

"Graaaaa —" the man moaned. As he stumbled closer, flecks of charred flesh dangled from his face. He reached out toward Cole with a hand that was burned through to the bone.

Cole turned and ran for the door, pushing aside anyone in his way. He could almost deal with dead people coming near him, but when they started to get aggressive, he knew it was time to leave.

But the man was close behind, his voice growing louder. "GRAAAAA . . . SEEEAL . . . A . . . FLESH!"

Leave me alone, Cole pleaded without saying a word. *Just leave me alone.*

"Nice talking to you!" Eddie called out.

But Cole wasn't listening. All he knew was that he had to get away.

FIVE

Detective Brown was at the Blacks' house when Cole and Jason returned.

He didn't have any news.

Ted was still missing without a trace.

Jason was deflated further by the news. Cole realized that Jason had honestly thought they could find Ted even when the police couldn't. Now Jason wasn't so sure.

Cole was prepared to stay around for the rest of the day. But then Mr. Black came home and a few more of the Blacks' friends brought over food. Suddenly the house was crowded and Cole felt like just one more intrusion. When Detective Brown offered him a ride home, he looked to Jason for an answer. Jason said he'd see him tomorrow in school.

The ride in Detective Brown's car was silent at

first. Cole could tell the cop had a lot going on in his mind. Suddenly, Cole realized why Detective Brown was taking the disappearances so hard. The cop's own older brother had suddenly disappeared when he was a kid. Detective Brown had told Cole this once because his brother had kept the same secret as Cole's; he, too, saw dead people. That's what had caused him to run away.

"What were you and Jason up to?" Detective Brown finally said, putting his private thoughts aside for a while.

"Looking for Ted."

The detective nodded. "I figured as much. No harm in that, as long as you're careful." He turned to Cole and stared hard at him for a second. "But there's something else, isn't there?"

Cole nodded.

"What is it?"

"It's one of the dead people," he whispered. It still seemed strange to say it aloud, to let it out instead of keeping it in.

"From the plane?"

"Yes."

"Do you know what he wants?"

"He's the one who keeps saying, 'It's all my fault.' I thought he was talking about the crash. But that's not it. It's something else."

"Do you know who he is?"

"Not his name."

"Well, there's one way to find out. Why don't we stop at the station?"

It was amazing to Cole how much he could leave unsaid with Detective Brown. Detective Brown already knew that the dead people only stayed around if they had something left to do. He already knew that the dead people came to Cole because they thought he could tie up the loose ends and bring them peace. Cole didn't have to go through the whole story every time he and Detective Brown talked. This made it much easier for both of them.

Back at the station, Cole left a message for his mom at home, telling her where he was. He wasn't supposed to call her at work unless it was really urgent — her boss was a maniac about avoiding personal calls on work time.

Detective Brown picked up a file from his desk. It contained photos of all the crash victims, from before they'd been in the crash.

"We need to find out who this guy is," Detective Brown explained. "And then hopefully we can figure out what he wants."

Cole told him about the whole scene at Grendel's, trying to remember every word.

Detective Brown glanced at his notes for a moment after Cole had finished. It was clear he had many questions. "So he said 'it's this way' and 'talk to her,' but he didn't say which way and he didn't say who he meant by 'her'?"

Cole shook his head. "His right arm sort of jerked when he said 'this way,' but that's about it. Then he made those sounds."

"'Grass seal a flesh'?" Detective Brown repeated. "Does that mean anything to you."

"No."

"Me neither."

He opened the file and slid a stack of photographs across the desktop. Cole looked at them carefully, one by one. These were the passengers of Flight 535 — all dead now. It made Cole so sad to think about that. He tried not to, because he knew that if started to think too much about death, he might never be happy again.

The guy with the missing ear seemed old but not ancient — maybe his mom's age, or a little older. But how could Cole be sure?

Cole narrowed the pile down to the men who seemed to have broad builds, like the burned man. Only one of them had reddish hair, turning gray. Passenger 49, George Daniel McMurphy of Cranville Falls, Iowa.

"This could be him," Cole said. "It's hard to tell."

Detective Brown examined the photo, then glanced down at the man's dossier. "Lived in the town for three years . . . stayed in the same job . . . no wife or kids. Very short obit — just got the page today. We know his birthday, but little else about his past. There's nothing really here about his life before he moved to Cranville Falls . . . which is not unusual for these small-town papers."

On the obituary page, Cole caught a glimpse of a small notice:

The employees of Alta Business Services
wish to express their regret
at the passing of their coworker,
George David McMurphy.
May he rest in peace.

"The middle name's different," Cole pointed out.

"They probably typed it in wrong," Detective Brown said with a sigh. "I'm afraid we're fresh out of clues."

The burned man's identity was still a mystery to Cole.

Cole thought he would get home before his mother. But no such luck.

"You didn't tell me about Jason's brother," she

said as soon as he came in the door. "I called over from work to see what time to pick you up, and Mrs. Black told me what had happened. I couldn't believe it. Then she told me you were with Detective Brown and I was even more confused. What's going on here, Cole?"

Cole told her the truth. Not the *whole* truth — he didn't tell her about biking to Grendel's, or the fight he'd almost been in. But he told her enough of the truth so that she would know what was going on.

"Oh, Cole," Lynn Sear said when he was finished telling her about Ted and the burned man. Her voice had shifted from irritation to concern. "I'm sorry I snapped at you. I had the worst day today — I thought I'd have the office to myself, but then Mr. Richardson showed up — no doubt trying to escape his awful, awful wife — and I couldn't get anything done. Every time I sorted something out, he'd un-sort it. I had to sneak into Dora's office to make a phone call. Then, to hear about Jason's brother . . . his poor parents. I offered to bring something over, but she said they were fine. You just can't imagine such a thing. But of course, you imagine it all the time."

Cole went over and gave his mother a hug. He knew that's what she needed.

"Thanks, hon," she said, pressing him close. If it was up to her, all the dead people would go away. If it was up to her, brothers and fathers would never leave.

But it wasn't up to her, or up to Cole, either. Instead they had to hold on to each other and find their way through.

SIX

News of the disappearances hit the newspapers the next morning. Five teens, all of them missing for more than a week. Ted's name wasn't mentioned. He hadn't been gone long enough yet.

Still, everyone at school knew. Mr. and Mrs. Black's frantic calls the night Ted went missing guaranteed that. Cole was impressed with Jason for showing up to class.

"It's much better than home," Jason confided. "The longer Ted's gone, the more afraid everyone gets."

Cole could understand that.

The day was frustrating — every hour meant another hour with Ted gone. The school rules had been bent so Jason could carry a cell phone. He and

Cole sat through every class hoping it would ring with good news . . . and dreading that it would ring with something worse.

At the end of school, Jason could barely stand still. He had to go look for Ted again.

"I talked to one of Ted's friends, Kent," he explained to Cole as they walked away from school. "He and some of Ted's other friends were going to form their own search party. I'm going to go along."

Three cars were waiting outside the high school building when Cole and Jason got there. Ted's friends and some other kids were crowding around.

"Hey, he's here!" shouted a tall kid with a duck-tail haircut. He sprinted to Jason. "We're all ready to go."

"Uh, I wasn't expecting the whole school to turn out for this, Kent," Jason said.

"It's for Ted. He needs us. Now come on, you're in my car. I called your mom and she said it was cool." Kent took Jason by the arm and pulled him toward one of the cars.

"I'll call you later!" Jason shouted to Cole.

His words were swallowed by the anxious buzz of the crowd. Cole tried to follow him, but it was useless. The kids were running every which way to get into the cars, as if preparing for a foreign invasion.

But not all of them were involved.

Standing against the wall of the school were a few kids watching the proceedings coolly, some of them shaking their heads in quiet disbelief.

One of them was Eddie.

Cole tried to duck away, but Eddie was on to him. "Hey, freak, where are you going?"

Freak.

Cole froze. He hadn't heard that word in what seemed like a long time. And he wasn't prepared for how it would make him feel.

He turned to face Eddie, his jaw and fists clenched. "What did you call me?"

Eddie ambled slowly across the lawn, which was quickly emptying as the cars sped away. "Tell me, do you always talk to yourself?"

"No," Cole said under his breath. Then he turned and began to leave.

"You know, I used to see Ted in all kinds of funky places," Eddie said quietly.

Cole stopped and turned back to him. "You did? Where?"

"Wherever there was trouble to be had," Eddie intoned in a mock radio announcer voice, then dropped it. "I bet you go for trouble, too."

Now Cole felt he was being teased.

Eddie must have sensed this. "Sorry," he said. "I bet you have your own problems, and you don't need me picking on you, too. Still, you have to lighten up a little. Live a little. Right now you look older than me. Way older."

Cole didn't know what to say to that.

"Check out the meat place," Eddie continued, giving Cole the address. "Be brave, and I promise you'll find something."

"What will I find?" Cole asked.

Eddie acted as if he hadn't heard the question. "In the warehouse — inside a big old meat locker, by the meat racks. Don't tell anyone else, and don't bring the police. Okay?"

Cole felt the cool, curious eyes of the other kids staring at him. He thought about asking Eddie further questions but decided against it.

The clue was good enough. He knew where he had to go.

He had to be brave.

Cole was lost in thought as the bus pulled into the depot.

"Missed your stop, kid?" the bus driver said jovially. "You can wait on the bus if you want. I'm leaving again in ten minutes."

"Thanks," Cole said, "but I'm getting off here."

He'd called his mom from a pay phone and had said he was with Jason.

Now he was alone in an unknown place.

Maybe he was as crazy as his dad.

He stepped off the bus, leaving the driver to puzzle it out.

The only people around were the warehouse workers, and they didn't pay much attention to Cole. He wound his way through the narrow streets, which seemed vaguely familiar. At each corner he could see the river, with its long, broken wharves reaching out like witches' fingers toward the sun.

His dad had worked down here in a shoe factory for a little bit, before it had been closed down and boarded up. Cole spotted the building and wondered if his loose-leaf snowflakes were still taped to his dad's old window. Sometimes his dad would take him on long walks among the bleak buildings, as part of their wanderings. The area was pretty decrepit back then, too, but Dad would describe all the old wholesale districts — the flower market, the fur trade, the meat and textile districts — and the streets would seem to come alive with the shouts of sailors and pushcart vendors and tradespeople.

Cole tried to remember where the meat district was. He turned into a long, vaguely familiar alley parallel to the dock.

He looked at the street sign.

Yes. This was it.

He walked slowly, staying close to the wall.

The building looked empty.

Crrack.

Cole stopped. The sound had come from inside.

"Ted?" he called out.

No answer.

He could make out a building entrance of some sort, just beyond a battered trash can. He approached carefully, guarding himself, preparing to run.

The door was blocked off, but there was plenty of room to crawl through.

Cole tried to push aside his own fear. He was doing this for Jason. He was doing this to find Ted. His heart thumped in his hollow chest.

In the last dull brush of sunlight, Cole could see the words carved into a white marble block above the entranceway.

GRAZIELLA FLEISCH
MEAT PURVEYORS
TO THE WHOLESALE INDUSTRY
PORK, BEEF, CHICKEN, VEAL

This had to be the place Eddie was talking about. Taking a deep breath, Cole stepped inside.

SEVEN

Frankie loves Rebecca.
The Clark Street Deuces Rule Forever.
Jake the Snake Wuz Here.

Cole read the messages on the warehouse walls as he walked along. Some of them had been written in tentative little hearts, some were announced with bold spray-paint swooshes. The warehouse was enormous, cold, and strewn with shredded plastic and metal parts. The smell of dead mouse was everywhere.

I promise you'll find something, Eddie had said. Cole hadn't doubted him. He'd taken Eddie at his word.

But what if Eddie had been making it up? Maybe sending Cole was his idea of a joke. A stupid prank to tease the freak.

It seemed to fit Eddie's personality.

Cole wanted to kick himself for being so easily fooled.

He turned back toward the entrance . . . and stopped cold.

Suddenly he knew.

They were here.

In the walls. In the floor.

Not just one.

Many of them.

And they knew Cole had arrived.

Cole turned and broke into a run along a shaft of light, his breath curling upward in wisps of white.

"You BURIED me. I wasn't lying to you, and YOU BURIED ME ALIVE!"

A man stepped into his path. His body was strangely compressed, as if someone very heavy had sat on him. Thick, grayish-white chunks weighed him down, clinging heavily to his hair and clothes. His feet were encased in the stuff, and when he walked they scraped along the floor.

"Buried alive," he repeated. *"Buried alive."*

The man was dead and angry. He didn't care that he'd probably been dead for decades. He didn't care that Cole was only a kid.

He just wanted revenge.

As the man moved further into the light, Cole

saw that the chunks were wet. And he realized what they were made of.

Cement.

As he realized this, two more dead people rose from the floor. They too were covered with cement.

They were coming from the foundation.

They were buried there. And nobody ever knew.

The first man lunged at Cole. He swung around — right into the arms of another.

"No!" Cole screamed. The dead person was surprised to get a reaction. He hesitated and Cole broke free, wet cement clinging to his clothes.

Cole ran into another room.

"HELP ME!" another man screamed, his stone-like arms swinging forward.

He didn't realize he was dead. He still thought there was a chance.

I can't, Cole thought. *I can't help you now.*

He began to call out Ted's name. Hoping he was here now. Hoping he could help.

"BURIED ALIVE . . ."

"HELP ME . . ."

The voices were getting louder. Cole saw a metal stairway and ran up the steps. He stumbled over debris and smashed into counters, feeling his way blindly . . . away . . . further into the darkness.

He collided with a thick metal door, covered on

the inside with shredded cloth padding. He could still hear their voices downstairs. He ran to the next room and pulled the door shut behind him.

This place smelled worse than the big room — a thick, rancid smell. A door in a distant wall was ajar, and Cole saw great, rusted hooks hanging from the ceiling on sliding racks. Meat hooks.

This was an old meat refrigerator, a locker.

It still felt cold.

Eddie had mentioned the locker. He had said Cole would find something here.

But there was no sign of Ted.

Cole heard footsteps on the stairs — the sound of cement shoes on metal.

They were coming for him.

It was a stupid idea to come here. A stupid, stupid idea.

Cole picked up the pace — but he stubbed his foot against a thick metal contraption and almost fell onto a meat hook. The moans below were a chorus of agony now.

How many people were buried here?

Cole struggled to his feet and hurtled toward the far door.

It was blocked.

By a body.

EIGHT

Cole cried out and fell back. His heel clipped a metal beam and he landed hard on the floor. He heard a crash — and the fading echo of another scream, not his own. A higher voice.

The body was a girl's.

She jumped up, immediately alert. She was Ted's age, with thin blond hair and fierce eyes.

She stared hard at Cole. "You're . . . a kid," she whispered. "What are you doing here?"

"I was just trying to go home," Cole said, scrambling to his feet.

"Don't go. Not yet."

Before Cole could reply, she slipped away into the shadows.

He followed after her hesitantly, his body in a cold sweat. She disappeared behind a curtain of sheets, strung up on meat hooks.

Through an opening he could see a small living arrangement — a sleeping bag, a ratty old blanket, a lopsided stack of shelves.

"You can come in," the girl said. "What's your name?"

"Cole."

Cole peered inside. The shelves were warped and broken. They held ancient-looking books and a tarnished mirror.

"You live here?" he asked cautiously.

"You might say that. Who are you?"

He saw other objects scattered around the curtained area. Lipstick tubes and candy bar wrappers. A few coins. A closed notebook. Cole couldn't tell how long they'd been there.

He spotted the glint of clear plastic behind two thick planks of wood. He reached in and pulled out a cassette tape with a bright, homemade orange label. On it was a list of songs, all written in a strange handwriting that slanted backwards all in capital letters.

"You found my mix tape!" the girl exclaimed. "Oh, Colin, you have saved my life."

Cole blushed. "Cole."

"Oops. So what are you doing here, *Cole.* Your mom and dad are probably freaking out."

"I just have a mom."

"Oh?" The girl nodded. "Me too. At least lately."

"I was looking for someone, but he's not here. His name is Ted Black. His brother is my best friend. Do you know him?"

"Can't say I do."

"Does that mean you can't say, or does that mean you don't?"

"Fussy kid, aren't you?" the girl said with a laugh that surprised them both. "And what makes you think you'll find this guy Ted here, anyway?"

"He's a runaway. Isn't that why you came here?"

The girl's smile faded. She sighed deeply and said, "You're very smart but, no offense, you're what, like eight? I'm not interested in discussing my life secrets with a kid."

Cole watched as she glanced at the things on the floor. She seemed really smart and pretty, the kind of high school kid who gets good grades and goes off to college. Cole wondered how she had gotten here. Ignoring her remark about him being just a kid, he said, "Can I ask you a question?"

"Depends on what the question is."

"Why do people run away?"

The girl let down her defenses a little. "Different reasons for different people, I guess. Something goes wrong and your life changes. Maybe everything feels stale, and you just want to run for air. Or maybe you suddenly realize that the life you've been leading and all the things you always took for granted are gone. And you can't live anymore with the people you once loved, because one of the things you took for granted was their love. And maybe it was never really there at all. Maybe you need to find it somewhere else. Maybe you're planning to make a life with someone new. Can you understand that?"

Cole thought about that for a minute. It made sense, kind of. Ted could have been feeling some of those things. But even if he felt them, that didn't mean they were right. His parents loved him.

Just like Cole and his mom loved his father.

But his father left anyway.

"I guess I better go," Cole said, turning to leave. Then a thought occurred to him. "You could come with me," he said to the girl. "Back to your home."

The girl became angry again.

"I can't do that, Cole. And you better not tell anyone where I am. Do you hear me? Because if you tell, I will make sure that I'm never found. Do you understand?"

Cole nodded.

"Promise?"

"Promise."

But Cole could tell she didn't really trust him.

He sensed that as soon as he left, she would move on.

Cole called Mrs. Black's cell phone from a corner pay phone. He was very relieved when Jason answered. Jason was still driving around in Kent's car. They hadn't found any clues that might lead to Ted.

"Where are you?" Jason asked.

"I'll tell you later," Cole said. "Just do me a favor and see if I can come over for dinner."

"I'm sure it's fine."

With his alibi intact, Cole caught the bus and headed to Jason's house. He got there just as Kent's car was pulling into the driveway. By the time they got to the front door, Mrs. Black thought they'd arrived together.

"Your mom just called, Cole," she said. "I told her you were staying for dinner. She's working late and will pick you up on the way home, at about eight."

Dinner at the Black house was really strained. Every time the phone rang, everyone would jump. But it was never the news they wanted to hear.

Cole sat in an extra chair at the table. Ted's chair remained empty.

"It just gets worse and worse," Mrs. Black said woefully.

"Don't talk like that," Mr. Black said, putting down his fork.

"Don't tell me how to talk, Peter," Mrs. Black replied.

"Mom. Dad," Jason said.

"Sorry, honey."

"Sorry."

Cole didn't say a word. He tried not to bolt from the table as soon as dessert was finished. Luckily, Jason quickly led the way upstairs.

"It's not always like this," Jason said as soon as they were alone in his room. "Now tell me where you were."

So Cole told him about the trip to the warehouse, leaving out the part about the men in cement. Jason listened, thunderstruck.

"Cole, I can't believe you did that. You should've told me. We all would've gone with you."

"But you had already driven away."

Jason looked at him head on. "Look — I don't want you to get in trouble, okay? It's bad enough with Ted gone. I don't want you to disappear, too."

This was the closest Jason had ever come to fully acknowledging their friendship. Even though he knew he was being warned, Cole also took some satisfaction in the force of Jason's words.

"I found a runaway," he said.

"In a cattle pen?"

"A meat locker. The thing is, Jason, you have to

promise not to tell anyone about her. Don't ask me why. I can't explain."

"Okay. Who is she?"

"I don't know."

"Did she know Ted?"

"I'm not sure. She said she didn't, but she might have been lying."

"Wait a sec." Jason ran into Ted's room and came back with a yearbook. "Maybe she went to school with Ted. Maybe she's in here."

Jason was grasping for anything — *anything* — that could lead to Ted. Cole understood. At dinner Mr. Black had said that with every passing day, the likelihood of Ted returning was less and less. He could be far gone by now. Or if something had happened to him — if he had been abducted off the street, or had a harmful accident — the more time went by, the less likely would be his chances of survival.

Sarah Abend . . . Jennie Arthur . . . Eve Billis . . . Cole looked at all of the girls in Ted's yearbook.

None of them matched.

"She might have been absent the day they took the photos," Jason pointed out.

"Yeah," Cole said. But they both knew he was agreeing without really meaning it.

They'd hit a dead end.

And Ted was still somewhere on the other side.

NINE

Cole's mom brought over a cake for Jason's mom. Cole wondered why people always brought over food at times like these. He remembered the days after his father had left. All his mother's friends brought over cookies and sweets. Neither Cole nor his mom felt like eating them. A week later, after most people had stopped coming by, they threw them all away.

Mrs. Black thanked Lynn for the cake, even though it looked a little . . . sad.

"The bakery was closing when I got there," Lynn explained to Cole when they got to the car. "It was the only one they had left. I just wanted to bring her something. Maybe I shouldn't have."

"I'm sure they'll like it," Cole reassured her.

"Sometimes it's so hard to figure out how to do the right thing," his mom said with a sigh.

As soon as the car turned on, the news radio station began its eight o'clock report.

"In our top story, police reports confirm that another teenager is missing from the Philadelphia area," the radio announcer blared. "His name is Ted Black, and his disappearance brings the total to six. A spokesperson for the mayor's office said that reports of kidnappings are premature, and that rumors of a grave found in a southern New Jersey landfill are absolutely false . . ."

"My God," Lynn said, shutting the radio off.

The car fell silent.

Cole stared out the window, looking at the faces of the people they passed. Even though he knew it was silly, he was hoping he'd find Ted this way. Just walking along the street. Waiting to be found.

"Did I ever tell you that I once tried to run away?" Lynn said to Cole. She asked it as a question even though she knew she'd never shared this story before. "I was fourteen. Your grandmother and I had the hugest fight. I can't remember what it was about — I remember the words I said, but I don't know why I said them. Probably she wouldn't let me go out when I wanted to go out. Something like that. But I told her that I hated her, and that I knew she hated me, too. She called me ungrateful and slammed my door so hard that I swear the whole house shook. My dad sat in the living room watching TV — he never got involved in our fights, and in my twisted logic I figured that this meant that he hated me, too. So I packed up a few things, left a note, and took off.

"Of course, I had no idea where to go. I knew they'd find me if I went to one of my girlfriends' houses. So I headed to the train station and swore to myself that I would take the first train out, no matter where it went. Well, the first train went to Miami, and I couldn't afford that. The second train went to Chicago, and I didn't want to go there because it was so cold. By the time the third train was boarding, I didn't know what I was doing. I was still so angry — but now I was as angry at myself as I was at my mother."

Lynn shook her head. "I was so stubborn. I didn't want to go back home, because I didn't want my mother to think I had backed down. I was about to buy a ticket to Boston when I saw her come through the station doors. She knew just where to find me. I saw her before she saw me. I saw that she was afraid — really terrified. And at that moment I realized how stupid I'd been. I realized how much she loved me."

Lynn looked out the windshield, but Cole knew she was seeing a memory of his grandmother — she was remembering coming home. "Now, let me tell you why I'm telling you this," she continued. "I know where Jason's brother is coming from, but I also know that he's wrong. He doesn't realize how much his parents love him, just like I didn't realize how much my parents loved me. There were a lot of things I didn't even realize until grandma and grandpa passed on. I don't want things to be like that with us. I don't want you to have to run away or for it to be too late in order for you to know how much I love you. Do you understand what I'm saying?"

Cole almost wanted to laugh. He had never doubted that his mother loved him. It was the one true, certain thing in his life.

"I'm not going anywhere," he said. "I know how much you love me."

"Good."

They drove on. Looking out the window now, Cole wasn't thinking only of Ted. He was thinking of all the runaways who were missing. He wished he could gather them all in one place and show them what their lives were really like. Show them the people left behind. Show them the love they'd left. Some of them might not be coming from loving homes — and in that case, Cole would want to help them find a better place. But for Ted and the others who were leaving good families behind — Cole wished he could talk to them and bring them back for one more chance.

It was a silly wish. As silly as wishing a father back home, or wishing for dead people to disappear.

But Cole hung on to it.

Somewhere there had to be hope.

TEN

Overnight, the city was covered with MISSING posters. Six young faces stared out from bulletin boards and shop windows.

HAVE YOU SEEN ME? the posters asked.

Below, the six missing runaways were frozen in time, caught in a family snapshot or a class picture. When they had sat for the photograph could they have possibly known that one day it would end up being used for this?

Cole didn't see the posters until he got to school. There they were, hung across the trophy case in the lobby. Cole's attention naturally turned first to Ted's face. Then, as he scanned the other posters, he let out a gasp.

There she was.

The girl from the meat warehouse.

She looked a little different, of course. Her hair was shiny and her smile gleamed. But there was no doubt in Cole's mind that it was her.

BRENDA MERCHANT, AGE 15.

Cole heard a cry from behind him.

He turned and found Mr. McMurphy, the burned man. He was staring at the MISSING posters, shaking with sobs.

Cole didn't understand it. He didn't understand it *at all*.

Jason wasn't in school that day. He and his family were going to join the other missing kids' families for a news broadcast that evening. All the local channels were going to air their plea, begging the runaways to come home.

Cole wondered whether there were TV's wherever Ted and the others were.

Or if Ted and the others were no longer . . . no, he wasn't going there.

Jason's other friends, who usually didn't spend much time with Cole, now came over to him and asked how Jason was doing.

Cole didn't know what to say. He couldn't tell them that everything was fine.

That would be a lie.

He couldn't concentrate in class. Every time he was in the hall, he would swing by the trophy case to look at Ted's and Brenda's faces. (He didn't recognize any of the other kids.) As the day went on, a plan formed in his mind. He knew what he had to do.

He had to see if Brenda was still in the warehouse. He had sworn to her that he wouldn't let anyone else know her location. But he hadn't promised that he wouldn't come back.

Mr. Richardson was keeping Cole's mom late at work again today — basically, she had to do all the filing she'd tried to do on Sunday before he interfered. Cole knew he had time to get to the warehouse and back. He just had to hope that Mr. Richardson would be watching over Lynn and she wouldn't get a chance to call home and check in.

After school, Cole ran to the bus stop and hopped on the first bus that came. As it made its way to the warehouse district, he thought about what he'd say to Brenda. The day before, she had dismissed him so easily. But things were different now.

He knew who she was.

He wouldn't threaten to tell other people about her location. He knew that wouldn't work — she'd follow through on her threat to disappear.

But he'd let her know what he'd found out. She'd know he was serious. Maybe she'd tell him about Ted.

If she knew anything.

The bus pulled into the depot. In the afternoon light, the waterfront seemed smaller and a bit less gloomy than last time — but not by much. Dark clouds were already crowding out the sun and the air smelled like rain.

As Cole made his way through the streets, he could hear the smack of the river current on the wood pilings.

A storm was coming.

He found the warehouse and entered cautiously. His breath didn't freeze this time.

The dead people weren't around.

Yet.

Cole's throat went dry as he made his way past the graffiti-covered walls. A mouse skittered frantically away, and something fluttered in the rafters above him.

He climbed the stairs cautiously. They were covered with clumps of cement.

The thick door to the meat locker was nearly closed. It took all of Cole's strength to pull it open enough to slide in.

"Hello?"

Cole's voice echoed into the high ceiling, unanswered.

In the corner where Brenda had been staying, the sheets now lay in a heap on the floor. The shelves had been torn down, and their contents strewn around. Magazines and books had been ripped to shreds. The sleeping bag was nowhere to be seen. The place was a wreck.

"Anybody here?" Cole shouted.

He ran out the back way, through the door where he'd discovered Brenda for the first time.

Nothing.

Then, from inside, he heard a faint noise.

Cole moved cautiously back into the big room. He thought he saw someone in the shadows . . . .

Click.

An overheard light sprung on. Cole was momentarily blinded.

"Brenda?" he asked.

"What can I get you, sir?" a deep voice said. "Pork loin or skirt steak?"

Cole recognized the voice immediately.

"Eddie?" he said. "What are you doing here?"

"Checking up on you," Eddie replied. "I thought you were after a Ted, not a Brenda."

"It's a long story," Cole said.

"Mm-hm. What if I were to tell you that I have some more information?"

"Last time, you made me think Ted would be here. Is this information any better?"

Eddie shuffled from foot to foot and plunged his hands into the pockets of his jacket, as if he had all the time in the world. "Maybe," was all he would say.

"Who are you, anyway?" Cole asked.

Eddie was heading out the door. "Are you coming or not?"

Cole thought about running the other way. He didn't trust Eddie. Was it a coincidence that he'd shown up here exactly when Cole had? Or had he been here all along?

Was he the reason Brenda was no longer here?

"You know Brenda, don't you?" Cole asked.

But Eddie was already in the street.

"I'd offer you a ride," he said, "but I'm afraid I've lost my car. We'll just have to walk."

Cole didn't know what to do. It seemed stupid to follow a guy like Eddie in a deserted neighborhood like this. But Eddie had tipped him off to this place — and he obviously knew more.

Cole thought of Ted's parents, and all the other parents, desperately waiting for their children to come home.

Suddenly, *not* going with Eddie seemed like a stupid thing to do.

So when Eddie headed off, Cole followed.

"I have to admit," Eddie said a few blocks later, "I totally underestimated you. Not many kids would do this for their friend's brother. You must have other reasons, too."

Now it was Cole's turn to stay silent.

Eddie laughed. "I'd never pegged you for a tough guy. Let me give you some advice. Stay tough, but never get too tough. Be willing to risk everything if you feel that's what you have to do. You might not come out ahead, but you'll sleep okay at night."

Let me give you some advice . . . Cole wondered if this was how Ted talked to Jason. He wondered if this was what it was like to have an older brother. Someone to tell you about all the things that were waiting ahead. Someone to show how to get through it all.

"What else?" Cole asked.

Eddie smiled. He was really liking Cole's company now. "Let's see — what else? If you tell a girl you love her, be prepared to stick with it. Don't ever wait until tomorrow to do something you want to do today, because you never know what tomorrow's going to be like. Never make promises you're not intending to keep."

As soon as Eddie said that, it started to rain. He didn't seem to notice until he saw his jacket turning dark with water.

"The bus!" he cried. Sure enough, there was one waiting at the stop. Cole and Eddie hurried to it.

Their next destination was Grendel's.

When they got to the arcade, it was much more jammed than before. Loud music boomed through enormous speakers. The floors shook under the weight of the bass. Crowds had formed around the video games, but no one seemed to mind much. Cole laid low, afraid he'd bump into Merv or someone like Merv.

He almost lost Eddie in the throng, but spotted him by the Coke machine. He turned briefly toward Cole, then vanished behind a black curtain, into the back room.

Dodging his way through the people, Cole reached for the curtain and pulled it back.

Inside was a dark room with walls that glowed with small pinpoints of light, as if Cole had launched himself into the middle of a galaxy. A round table sat in the middle, covered in black velvet and supporting a small globe that pulsated with miniature blue lightning bolts.

A group of teenagers sat around the table, each fingering a deck of luminescent cards. Eddie stood on one side.

On the other side, a stranger slowly stood up.

All Cole could see of him at first was the back of his shaved head. When he turned, his teeth and eyes seemed to radiate fluorescent light.

He wasn't smiling, exactly. His face was fixed in an uncomfortable grimace, which made Cole feel like apologizing, even though he didn't really have anything to apologize for. Really, Cole wanted to bolt to the safety of home. But it was way too late for that.

"This is Spider," Eddie said. "He'll take care of you."

"S-Spider?" Cole repeated.

"He's heard of you!" one of the kids said with a laugh.

Spider stepped closer. He was bone-thin, with a small ring in his right ear and a bladelike beard. His shirt glowed with the outline of a hideous creature — a dark, poisonous-looking tarantula with a rodent-like face and eight legs that ended in knives.

"What do you want?" he said in a small, oddly wispy voice.

"Do you know Ted Black?" Cole asked nervously.

Spider squinted. "Ted *who*?"

"How about Brenda Merchant?" Cole pressed on. "Do you know her?"

"What are you talking about?" Spider spat.

As he did, Cole noticed two of the other guys turning away.

They knew something.

"Eddie said you could tell me things —" Cole blurted out, stopping himself to glance desperately at Eddie.

"Tell him the truth, Spider," Eddie said.

"Like what?" Spider said flatly.

One of the other guys at the table turned to Cole. "What's up, little man?" he said. "Are you a runaway, too? Why don't you go home and ask your mom to pack you a couple of peanut butter sandwiches before you head underground?"

"Enough!" Spider yelled. Then he calmed down again. "I'm afraid we can't help you," he said to Cole before opening a door in the back of the room and stepping out.

"Wait —" Cole said.

Eddie shrugged. "He never listens. Guess we have to work on our conversation skills. Let's go."

Immersed in their card game, none of the other guys looked up.

"Spider has spoken," Eddie intoned.

Cole headed dejectedly back through the black curtain.

As he walked back through the arcade, he saw the guy he'd seen before — the one he'd thought was Ted.

Up close, he didn't look anything like Ted.

Nothing was right anymore.

Cole still got home before his mother, who ended up having to work until nine, which she was *not* very happy about. Alone, Cole watched the families of the runaways on TV. Ten minutes after the news was through, Jason called.

"Did you see it?" he asked.

Cole told him he had.

"It was so strange. You know that girl Brenda? Well, it ends up that her brother Ben was on my soccer team last year. Isn't that weird?"

As Cole fell asleep that night, the burned man reappeared.

He was still crying and moaning.

All he could ask was, *Where is she?*

These are the words Cole fell asleep to.

In the morning he thought about Jason's connection to Brenda's brother, Ben.

And he came up with a plan.

ELEVEN

Cole and Jason headed across town to the Merchants' apartment after school. This time they didn't have to lie to their mothers about where they were going. Jason said he wanted to catch up with Ben, especially considering the current situation. Cole said he'd been asked along.

Cole hadn't been able to fully explain his hunches to Jason, but Jason didn't seem to mind. He was willing to take his friend at his word. And he was willing to follow any lead that might bring his brother back home.

"So many people called after the news broadcast," Jason said on the way. "Our number is in the phone book, after all. Old friends of my parents. People from their jobs. And plenty of weirdos. People said they'd seen Ted abducted — by criminals, or by aliens. People said they thought they saw someone who might look like Ted in a Wal Mart in Scranton, or a sport store in Cherry Hill. But none of it came to anything, and Mom started getting frantic that the line was being tied up, so if Ted was trying to call, he wouldn't get through. We have call waiting, but that only takes two calls at a time. Last night it wouldn't stop ringing."

Cole saw the toll this was taking on his friend. The sleepless eyes. The ragged edges of his chewed-down fingernails.

And the fear now coming to the surface.

"I don't know, Cole," Jason said shakily. "I really thought Ted would be home by now. I know he wanted to leave. I know he felt things were messed up here. But I thought he'd leave for a couple of days, prove his point, and come back. Or at least call us to let us know he was okay. To make Mom and Dad and me worry like this is *mean*. And it's not like Ted to be that mean. I think something's happened to him. I think something really bad has happened to him."

Cole didn't know what to say. So instead he quoted someone else.

"Detective Brown says it's going to work out," he assured Jason. "He's seen hundreds of cases like this, I bet. We can trust him."

"I hope so," Jason replied. He didn't sound entirely convinced.

The Merchants lived on the third floor of an apartment building that smelled like an old sock. Their apartment was up three flights of creaky wooden stairs, at the end of a narrow hallway.

The door opened as they approached, revealing a kid their own age.

"Hey, Ben," Jason said. "This is Cole."

Cole shook his hand. Ben had the same tired look as Jason. They were both suffering hard.

"Come in," Ben said, leading them into the living room.

Ben seemed uncertain about why Jason and Cole had come, even though they'd called ahead.

"I don't know if I can help you," he said. "I mean, we told the police everything about Brenda. And I don't think she knew your brother, did she?"

Jason looked to Cole for an answer.

"We're not sure," Cole said.

"I'm sorry my mom isn't here," Ben went on. "She might be able to help you more. She's with Detective Brown right now, going over things. Ever since the TV show, a lot of people have called. She's sorting through what they said."

"That happened to us, too," Jason said.

"Is your father here?" Cole asked. And as soon as he said it, he knew what he'd done. Ben's face froze — half angry, half sad. Cole knew that look . . . from the inside. So he knew what Ben was going to say next.

"My dad isn't around. He left when I was eight."

"Mine left when I was seven," Cole said.

"Really?"

"Yeah."

"It sucks, doesn't it?"

"Yeah, it sucks."

Ben seemed slightly more comfortable. "Brenda was older, so she took it harder, you know?"

Cole remembered what Brenda had said in the warehouse — something about what happened when the things you took for granted were suddenly gone. As she'd said that, Cole had thought of his father. Now he knew that Brenda was thinking about her father, too.

"Have you heard from him?" Cole asked.

Ben shook his head. "He kind of disappeared. So I guess you could say this has happened to us before. We were supposed to meet him at the ballet. It was Brenda's favorite thing to go to. I hated it, but I went anyway. So we got there and we waited for him to show up. He never did. We went to the ballet anyway, and when we got home, a lot of his stuff was gone. He left a note and said he'd be in touch. He said he was sorry, and that he'd make it up to us some day. Or at least that was what Mom says was in the note. She burned it as soon as she read it, she was so mad.

"Then Brenda left, and she didn't even leave a note. We searched everywhere for one. Mom thought she might have been kidnapped. But she'd taken some of her things. It's so strange, because she was so angry at Dad for leaving. I can't believe she'd do the same thing unless she had a really good reason."

"Are you sure there wasn't a reason?" Cole asked gently.

"I don't think so. I mean, Mom was getting stricter and stricter. She didn't want Brenda going out, especially after Brenda started hanging with these older boys. That drove Mom crazy. They'd fight a lot. But it's not like Brenda hated it here. I would've known. I swear, I would've known."

Cole looked at Jason. He knew his friend felt the same way about Ted.

"Do you hear from your father?" Ben asked Cole.

"Not really," Cole answered truthfully. "He's called a few times. Once he called after he got into a fight with his new girlfriend. Mom says he was feeling sorry for himself, so he called us to feel even sorrier. Mom let me get on the phone, but I didn't really have anything to say to him."

"At least you know where he is," Ben pointed out.

"But that almost makes it worse," Cole confided. "Because you know he still exists. Which means he's choosing not to see you."

Cole was getting distracted. He hadn't come here to talk about his own problems. But it felt good to be with someone who sort of understood.

"My mom says that you say you hate someone because you don't want to feel the pain of loving him so much," Ben spoke up. "She says that Brenda was trying to convince herself to hate him so it wouldn't feel so bad anymore."

"That doesn't work," Cole said sympathetically.

"I know. But I don't think Brenda knows that. Mom thinks she might have run away to find him, so she could tell him how much she hated him. I think she ran off for another reason — to meet some guy, or just to get away. But I really don't know."

Cole was struck by how whole lives could change in one day. Ben and Brenda came home from the ballet and found their father gone. Cole got home from school and found his mom crying at the kitchen table, clutching his father's note. Mr. and Mrs. Black checked Ted's room in the middle of the night and saw he wasn't in his bed, where he was supposed to be. One moment in one day could turn a person's life forever into a Before and an After.

Jason and Ben started to talk about being on TV. They made fun of one of the newscasters, who had to have his mustache brushed for him before he went on the air. Cole suddenly felt very tired. He decided to go to the rest room.

"Second door on the right," Ben told him. "Just past Brenda's room."

Cole slipped into the bathroom and moved to the sink. He ran the water and splashed it over his face. It was cold, incredibly cold, and it made him feel better. He took a few deep breaths, straightened his hair, and headed back out.

For the first time, he noticed Brenda's room.

He stopped. It was neat, decorated carefully. Posters covered the wall, the spaces between them filled with old prize ribbons and framed photographs. A Calder mobile hung from the ceiling.

Somewhere in here, he realized, there might be a clue to why Brenda left.

He listened briefly to the conversation that filtered in from the living room; Jason and Ben were still talking about being the brother of a missing kid. Ben mentioned that some of Brenda's friends had been "trouble." Jason said his parents believed the same thing about Ted's new friends.

Neither of them were missing Cole. Yet.

Silently, he slipped into Brenda's room.

It was stuffy and smelled of perfume and hidden cigarettes. Her closet jammed with clothes.

Cole's eye was drawn to her dresser. Several photos had been tucked into the frame of her mirror. Brenda and a woman who must be her mom at Disney World. Brenda as a little girl on Santa's knee. Brenda swinging on a tire, being pushed by the hand of some unseen man. Brenda as a teen in the center of a grubby-looking group of kids.

He tiptoed around her bed and approached the mirror. In the image he could see that her door was half open, exposing him to the hallway.

He turned to close the door.

And it moved.

Cole swiftly ducked behind the dresser. Heavy footsteps entered the room. Cole felt cold and saw his breath.

He stood up and faced the man with the burned-off ear.

Mr. McMurphy.

"What are you doing here?" Cole asked.

The man said nothing. He lifted his arm as if to grab Cole, but stopped short. His hand just dangled downward, as if it had stopped working.

Cole realized he was pointing.

Cole followed the angle of the arm to Brenda's top drawer. He reached tentatively for it and tried to pull it open.

The drawer was jammed shut, so he gave it a good, hard yank. It flew open, spilling girls' underwear all over the floor.

Cole jumped back.

Now *this* was gross.

Was he actually supposed to reach in to the remaining underwear and find something? Cole glanced at the man pleadingly, but he was still pointing.

Holding his breath, Cole dug his hands inside the drawer. He pushed aside underwear until he felt something different — a small spiral notebook.

He pulled it out by the spine. Two small photos fell out and fluttered facedown to the carpet.

Cole stooped and picked them up.

The first was a shot of Brenda on some school campus, laughing out loud, her arms draped around a kid in a green jacket.

Cole held the image close to Brenda's nighttable light, until he could make out the boy's face.

His hand shook.

It was Eddie.

Cole turned the photo over and read the date. About a month ago. It was written in a handwriting

Cole recognized, the capital letters slanting backwards.

The same handwriting as on Brenda's tape.

So Eddie *had* known Brenda. They'd been a couple.

Why hadn't he told Cole?

Maybe the other photo would give a clue. Cole turned it over and held it to the light. This one was older, dogeared and bent. It showed Brenda, much younger, arm in arm with a smiling man.

Her father.

He looked familiar, probably because he looked like Brenda. The darker, more intense side of Brenda.

There was something else, though. Something about the set of his jaw, the way his head was tilted, his reddish hair and coloring.

Then it hit Cole.

He looked into the mirror.

The burned man was gone.

But his face was still in the photo.

TWELVE

"Cole!" Jason's voice called out.

Cole could barely hear him, there were so many thoughts yelling in his mind.

Her father.

The burned man was Brenda's father.

The one who left.

How was this possible?

What did it mean?

Everything Cole knew about the man instantly changed.

He *was* here for a reason, that was clear.

He needed something — and it had nothing to do with the plane crash. It had to do with his family.

With Brenda.

But what?

"Yo, Cole, are you all right?"

Jason made Cole snap back to reality.

He couldn't be found in Brenda's room. There would be too much explaining to do.

He stuffed the two photos back into the notebook, hastily put the notebook and the underwear back in the drawer, and slammed the drawer shut. Making sure he hadn't disturbed anything else, he left the room.

Reaching across the hall, he pulled the bathroom door open and shut, so Ben and Jason would hear it.

"I'm fine!" he yelled.

When he got back to the living room, Ben said, "We thought you'd fallen in."

Jason groaned. "My dad says that."

"Mine did, too," Ben said.

There were so many questions Cole wanted to ask — but where could he start? Obviously, Ben didn't know his dad was on Flight 535.

He didn't know his dad was dead. And he didn't know where Brenda really was.

A key sounded in the front door's lock, and the knob turned. Brenda's mother walked in . . . with Detective Brown. As Ben introduced Cole to his mother, the detective looked at Cole curiously. *What are you up to?* he eyes asked. But Cole knew he wouldn't say anything aloud, not with Ben, Jason, and Mrs. Merchant in the room. So he was safe . . . for now.

The time to ask Ben questions had passed. Now that his mom was in the room, he fell silent as she talked about what Brenda was like as a child. Detective Brown nodded sympathetically, but he didn't need to take any notes.

After a few minutes, one of Mrs. Black's friends came by to pick up Jason and Cole. As Jason walked ahead to the car, Detective Brown excused himself from the Merchants and pulled Cole aside.

"What's going on, Cole?" the detective asked as soon as they were out of the apartment.

Cole didn't know how much to say and how much to leave out.

In the end, he whispered, "Ask Mrs. Merchant to see a picture of Mr. Merchant."

Detective Brown shot him a quizzical look. But instead of questioning the boy, he nodded.

"I gotta go," Cole said, gesturing in the direction that Jason had already gone.

Detective Brown nodded again, and said no more.

Jason and Cole couldn't talk in the car. So when they got to Cole's house, Jason pretended he needed to borrow a book. Mrs. Black's friend was willing to wait for a minute while he went inside to get it.

Jason didn't know it, but he was the first friend to visit Cole's house in a very long time. Usually it was too dangerous — at first, Cole could never be sure what kind of mood his mom would be in, since she was so sad and angry after his dad left. Then, when the dead people started crashing in more and more, Cole didn't want people over . . . because he didn't want people to see him so scared.

Now he thought he could handle it.

For a few minutes, at least.

Cole's mom wasn't home yet. Instead she was represented by the flashing red light on the answering machine — working late again, no doubt.

"Why were you in the bathroom so long?" Jason asked when they got inside.

"Actually, I was checking out Brenda's room," Cole admitted.

"Whoa. Did you find anything?" Jason was impressed — and scared.

"Not really," Cole lied. There was no way he could explain. Not yet.

"Well, I talked to Ben about where Brenda hung out. I was hoping she'd have someplace in common with Ted. But Ben didn't think she hung out at Grendel's, or in our neighborhood. Listen to this, though. He told me that Brenda's a movie nut. She likes to go to the multiplex near our school and stay there all day, going from show to show. Sometimes she would take a couple of different jackets to fool the ushers."

"Did Ben tell this to the police?"

"Sure. But I don't think they've checked in a while. I think we should go there and see."

"Not now, right? It's dinnertime."

"Of course not," Jason said, although Cole could tell that he'd really wanted to go right away. "Tomorrow after school. Deal?"

"Deal." Cole didn't see how he could say no.

Cole's mom came home about a half hour after Jason left. Dinner was going to be very late.

"I'm sorry, honey," she said. But she looked too tired to be really sorry. She looked like she wanted to crawl into bed and go to sleep right away. "I swear to God, I'm not a violent person. But if I could make the ground open up beneath Mr. Richardson's feet and have it swallow him up . . . well, let's just say I'd really be tempted to do it. Do you want to know the reason I'm late? He had me spend an hour on his computer looking for a file he swore he'd lost. Then, long after it was time for me to leave, he realizes that the file is on his *home* computer. He doesn't even thank me for searching. He just looks at his desk and says, 'That will be all.' The nerve of the man! If I didn't need this job, I would be so far out of there, Cole."

"I know, Mom."

"But listen to me venting. How was your day?"

Before Cole could answer, the doorbell rang.

Detective Brown burst in as soon as Lynn opened the door.

He was holding a photo of Mr. Merchant.

"Are you saying what I think you're saying, Cole?" the detective asked.

"Whatever happened to 'hello, how are you'?" Lynn commented.

Detective Brown brushed her aside with his hand. This *really* annoyed her.

"Yes. It's him. Isn't it?" Cole replied.

"Would someone tell me what's going on here?" Lynn insisted, turning on Detective Brown. "Do *all* of your cases involve my son, or is it only just the ones that make the news?"

"I'm sorry, Lynn —"

"You can call me Ms. Sear — 'Lynn' was only for when you were being polite."

"I'm sorry, *Ms. Sear*, but Cole has stumbled onto something really big."

"But how does it help?" Cole asked. This was

what had been worrying him — it was certainly a big deal that Mr. McMurphy was really Mr. Merchant, but it didn't get them any closer to finding out about Brenda.

"I don't know," Detective Brown admitted. "I'm going back to the station now to try to piece things together. I don't want to tell Ben and Mrs. Merchant about Mr. Merchant until we're a hundred percent sure. It's going to be another big shock for them."

Cole could see his mom was still confused. "One of the dead people is also one of the runaway's father," he said.

Lynn paused for a moment. There were many things she wanted to say, but in the end she went with, "Does he know what happened to him — or her?"

Cole shook his head.

"And is the dead father here now?" Lynn asked.

Cole shook his head again.

Lynn sighed, relieved.

But Cole wasn't through with Mr. Merchant yet.

THIRTEEN

Sometime after midnight, long after Detective Brown had returned to the station and Lynn had fallen into an easy sleep, Cole sat up quietly in bed.

"Mr. Merchant . . ." he whispered.

Cole waited for the cold to come, but it didn't. The room was warm, stifling. Cole threw back the covers and stood in the middle of the floor.

"Mr. Merchant, I want to talk to you now . . ."

Nothing. No sound, no movement.

Cole couldn't believe it. When he hadn't wanted to see the burned man, he'd always been around. Now that he had something to say, Mr. Merchant was nowhere to be found.

He tried three times . . . four.

"It's for Brenda!" he yelled.

A half hour passed.

Cole would not go to sleep until this was through.

Finally, there was cold. There was movement in the darkness.

Cole waited.

As Mr. Merchant shuffled into view, Cole tried to find some pity. This man had died unexpectedly in a plane crash. His daughter had run away. Cole knew he should feel sorry for him.

But mostly, he felt angry.

This man had abandoned his family.

This man had never written, never called.

This man had started another life, totally ignoring the people he left behind.

Now he didn't say a word. He looked around Cole's room and started to leave.

"Not yet," Cole said, standing in Mr. Merchant's way. "I have to talk to you first."

Mr. Merchant stopped. For the first time, he looked straight at Cole.

"You want to help Brenda, right?" Cole asked. "You know, *your daughter.*"

The dead man nodded.

"Well, maybe that's something you should have thought about before, when you *left her.*"

Cole remembered his own father's note in his

mother's hand. He remembered the weeks and month and years that followed — all those hard times, all those moments when the house seemed empty, broken.

"Why did you do it?" he asked Mr. Merchant. "Did you think she'd just get over it? You're worried about her now, but were you worried about her for all those years you didn't contact her?"

Cole couldn't believe he was saying so much. But the words wouldn't stop — they had a life of their own. They'd been trapped inside for years, waiting for a chance to be heard.

"You keep saying it's all your fault," he said. "Well, maybe it *is* all your fault. You say that you hurt them. Well, maybe you have *no idea* how much you hurt them. If you're here because Brenda's gone and you think you can help find the runaways, then you better start helping me. If you're here for another reason, then I'm not going to help you. The runaways are more important."

"*I know,*" Mr. Merchant moaned. "*I know.*"

Cole had to ask the one question he'd always wanted to ask his own father.

"Are you sorry?"

Mr. Merchant nodded. "Yes."

"Then . . . why? Why did you leave?"

"I had to," Mr. Merchant said quietly. Now that

he knew Cole was connected to his family — now that he knew Cole wanted to help — he found more strength to speak. "I was in a . . . bad business deal. I had to borrow money from . . . bad people. Crooks. I couldn't pay them back. They were going to come after me . . . hurt my family. I had to . . . disappear. I couldn't let anyone trace me. I had to be . . . someone else."

"George McMurphy," Cole said.

"Yes. I waited . . . wanted to come back. But I had someone here . . . in Philadelphia . . . he told me I was still in danger. I stayed away. Then I heard about . . . Brenda."

"That she was missing?"

"Yes. I knew I had to . . . help. On the plane, all I could think was . . . what I did to them." If I found her, I could make it up to all of them.

And then the plane crashed.

He never had a chance.

Suddenly Cole felt more sad than angry. He imagined Mr. Merchant on the plane, flying back to help Mrs. Merchant find Brenda. Maybe planning his apologies. Maybe planning to come back.

But by then it was too late.

The family would never know for sure. They would find out that he'd been on the plane. They might figure out that he'd come for them. But they would never see him again. They would never get to see the regret in his eyes, or hear the words "I'm sorry" come from his lips.

Even if Cole told them, they'd never really know.

"Do you know where the runaways are?" Cole said.

Mr. Merchant shook his head slowly. "Gone . . . Brenda . . ."

"My best friend's brother is gone, and other kids are gone, too. Brenda might be the clue to lead us to them."

"My daughter is . . ."

"Can you help me?"

"It's all my fault."

"Brenda might be your fault, but the others aren't. You can help Mr. Merchant."

"I don't see her!"

The sound of footsteps made Cole jump.

"Cole?" his mom was calling. "Are you okay?"

Cole spoke to the closed door. "I'm fine!"

"I heard talking. Were you talking to someone?"

"Sort of. But not anymore."

"Sort of?" Lynn pushed the door open and peered inside.

Cole turned to tell Mr. Merchant to stay.

But he was already gone.

"What's going on, Cole?" Lynn asked.

"I can't sleep," he replied.

Lynn gave him a weary smile. "Insomnia Cafe, open for business. You want something to eat?"

"No, I'm okay."

"Okay." Lynn pulled her bathrobe tighter around her body and headed back to her room. But before she left the hall, Cole stopped her with a question.

"Do you still miss him, Mom?"

Lynn looked a little surprised by the question, but she wasn't going to withhold a truthful answer.

"Of course I miss him sometimes."

"Do you want him to come back?"

Lynn shook her head. "No, Cole. I don't want your father to come back. It would never work. You know that, don't you?"

Cole did know that. But still a small part of him wished it wasn't true.

"Where are these questions coming from, Cole?" his mother asked gently. "Did you have a nightmare?"

"I was thinking about how Brenda Merchant's father left her family, too," Cole explained.

Lynn came over and put her arms around Cole. "A lot of people get left," she said, holding him tight and putting her forehead on his. "The bad news is that it hurts real bad and turns your life into a total mess. The good news is that most people survive and are stronger than before. What your father did was the worst thing anyone's ever done to me. But the two of us surviving has been the best thing that ever happened to me. So it evens out, Cole. You have to believe that."

"I do," Cole whispered.

He knew that he and his mom had survived.

He hoped the Merchants would do the same.

He would have to help them.

FOURTEEN

The next morning, the news announced another teenager was missing. A fifteen-year-old honor student, the co-captain of the city's championship basketball team.

The newscaster, Zach Simko, said the police effort was "intensifying."

But still, there weren't any new clues.

When Cole's mom was safely in another room, he called Detective Brown and told him what Mr. Merchant had said. The detective thanked him curtly and got off the phone. Clearly, the pressure at the police department was intensifying along with their efforts.

Detective Brown sounded stressed.

With the lives of seven runaways on his shoulders, Cole could understand why.

Cole headed with Jason to Brenda's favorite multiplex hangout after school. He couldn't think of anything better to do.

"Just how old *are* you?" the ticket taker asked skeptically as Jason shoved money through the hole in the Plexiglas booth.

"Thirteen," Jason said.

"Eleven," Cole piped up at the same time. *Oops.*

"Fatal Conflict is PG-13." The ticket taker slid back the money. "You could both see *The Enchanted Frog.* It's rated G."

"Okay," Jason said, grimacing. "Two for that."

As they took their tickets and walked inside, Jason shot Cole a look. "I am so embarrassed . . . I can't believe we just bought tickets for *The Enchanted Frog.* Next time say you're thirteen, okay?"

"We don't actually have to *watch* it," Cole reminded him.

"Right," Jason said as they scooted down to the lower level of the multiplex. "Now which film would Brenda Merchant be watching?"

They decided to split the theaters and look for Brenda.

"Here," Jason said, taking out the cell phone he'd been carrying. "Take this. My parents got me a pager. I programmed the number in the cell phone, so if anything happens, you can beep me."

Cole thought the idea of a kid his age having a cell phone and a pager was pretty silly. But he could understand why the Blacks would be overprotective of Jason, considering what was going on with Ted.

Cole put the phone in his pocket.

"I'll start with *Fatal Conflict.* You can do *Pure Sunshine.* Just wait until the ushers' backs are turned and pretend you belong." Jason checked his watch. "I'll meet you in the men's room in a half hour or so. But beep me if something happens first."

"What if we find Brenda? We can't really bring her in the men's room."

"The lobby, then. Good luck."

As Jason headed away, Cole slipped into the first theater. In a half hour, he figured he might even have a chance to double-check the theaters Jason was going into. He wished Jason hadn't come — but since it had been Jason's idea, he was out of luck.

The first movie was in full swing, but only a dozen or so people were there, none of them Brenda. He tried a movie called *I Will Survive* next — it was pretty funny, but still no Brenda.

The theater for *Northern Lights* was empty. And cold.

Cole stared at the screen. The idea of a movie playing to no people — the actors crying and freezing in the snow, people falling in and out of love, even when no one was watching — was strangely beautiful. Even though it wasn't the kind of movie Cole liked, he took off his backpack and sat for a moment. He could hear the whir of the projector and he could see the ray of images that hit the screen. It was very peaceful in here.

After a few lost minutes, Cole got up to leave.

As he stood, he heard a sound.

A sniffle.

From the front.

Cole quietly sidled out to the aisle and tiptoed forward.

In the second row, he saw a figure slouched down in a seat, wearing a T-shirt, ink-marked jeans, and a dark coat. Blond hair cascaded over the coat's collar.

In the flickering light of the movie, Cole saw the empty sadness in Brenda's eyes.

"Brenda?" Cole whispered.

She turned to him, startled out of her reverie. "What the —?"

Cole looked at her jeans and saw she'd written on them. An eight-legged insect with the face of a rodent.

The same shape as the one on Spider's T-shirt.

"I — I have to ask you a question," Cole began.

"Are you *crazy*?" Brenda bolted up from her seat. "What are you doing here? Why are you following me?"

"I need your help —"

"Oh, and you think you'll get it by chasing me down in movie theaters, stalking me in the warehouse, and telling people where I am?"

"I didn't tell anybody!" Cole protested. He couldn't imagine that Jason counted.

"Well, maybe you can explain how they found me, then?"

"*Who* found you?"

Brenda shook her head in disbelief. "I didn't think they'd send someone so young," she said. "I have to hand it to Thorn. He caught me off guard. I'm lucky I got out of the warehouse before he found me. But it's not going to happen again."

"I don't know what you're talking about," Cole insisted. "Who's Thorn?"

"Aren't you a little young to be a runaway? Go home, Cole — if that's even your real name. Go home while you're still free."

"I'm not a runaway," Cole said. He decided to try a different approach. "I saw your mom, Brenda. I saw her and Ben. They both miss you."

Brenda seemed to back down a little. A glimmer of doubt flickered in her eyes — but she countered it with more hostility. "Well, I miss them, too. You can tell Thorn that. But I haven't gone back — tell him that, also. Tell him I'm still waiting for someone. And tell him to leave me alone. I'm paying the price. His secret is safe with me."

"What secret?"

Brenda studied his face. "If you don't actually know what I'm talking about, I'm getting you into more trouble than you deserve. And if you *do* know what I'm talking about, I'm getting myself into more trouble than *I* deserve."

"Tell me," Cole pleaded.

"Sit down and I'll tell you."

Cole sat in one of the theater chairs and waited for the explanation to start.

"Here's the deal," Brenda said, standing between Cole and the aisle. "This is good-bye."

With that, she dashed from the theater.

Cole jumped up and tried to follow. But he was taken by surprise. And she was too fast.

"Wait!" Cole shouted. "I have to talk to you!"

He ran after her — but when he reached the lobby, she was gone.

Cole ran to the stairs, just as Jason exited *Life-*

guards II. "Don't bother," Jason said. "That is the worst movie ever made."

Then Jason noticed Cole was out of breath from running.

"What is it?" he asked.

Cole didn't know what to say. He had gotten into this whole situation because of Jason and his missing brother.

But now, all of a sudden, he didn't want Jason to be involved.

It was getting too dangerous.

And too complicated.

"Nothing," Cole replied, a half second too late.

"You're hiding something, aren't you?" Jason said.

"No."

"Did you see her?"

"Not really."

"*'Not really'?* What does *that* mean, Cole?"

"It means no."

Jason started looking around the lobby, sprinting to the front of the theater and out onto the sidewalk. Cole followed close behind, even though he knew it was too late. Jason wouldn't find her.

"You let her get away, didn't you?" Jason accused. "She was the only hope we had, Cole."

That's not true, Cole wanted to say. But that would get Jason involved even deeper.

"You should've beeped me! You should have blocked her or screamed my name or something."

"It wouldn't have worked," Cole said. He knew that Jason wasn't just angry at him. He was angry at the whole world right now.

"I shouldn't have brought you along," Jason said. "I should've looked myself. I'm going home now."

It was clear from Jason's tone that Cole was *not* invited to join him.

So Cole watched as his best friend set off for his house — it wasn't that long a walk away. Cole knew he'd disappointed him . . . but he didn't see any way around it.

He just knew some things Jason didn't know, that's all.

Cole stood for a moment outside the theater, feeling stung. After Jason was out of sight, he turned away and headed back to his own house, paying no attention to the rush of people sweeping by him.

At the playground down the block from the multiplex, a group of boys played basketball. They looked high-school age, and Cole instinctively looked up to see if Ted was among them.

Instead he saw Eddie, leaning against the chain-link fence, hands in his pockets.

Cole waved, but Eddie seemed not to see him. He zipped his jacket up tighter and walked across the playground.

"Hey!" Cole shouted, breaking into a run. Now that he knew Eddie was connected to Brenda for sure, there were a million questions he wanted to ask.

By the time he got around the fence, Eddie had vanished around a street corner. Cole chased after him, darting through the rush hour throngs that now poured out of the buildings.

Across the street, sitting on a park bench, Eddie smiled at him and winked.

Cole sprinted across, in the midst of a crowd, but now Eddie was a half block away, walking briskly into an electronics store.

Cole ran into the shop, panting heavily. It was a cramped, unfriendly place, with a theft detector at the door and a huge sign hanging from the ceiling that SHOPLIFTERS WILL BE SEVERELY PUNISHED.

A clerk, arranging batteries on a rack, gave him an appraising look. "Can I help you?"

"No, thanks," Cole said. "Just looking."

Eddie was at the end of the center aisle, surrounded by racks of cordless phones. As Cole approached, he slipped away behind the shelves.

He's enjoying this, Cole thought.

Cole couldn't find him in the next aisle, or the next. Then, out of the corner of his eye, he saw a movement in the back of the store. He tiptoed in that direction and quietly peeked around the shelf.

Suddenly he felt a presence behind him.

"Boo!" Eddie said into his ear.

Cole spun around. Eddie was racing out of the store.

This was a big game to him — and Cole was going to try to beat him at it.

Cole ran full tilt to the front. He had let Brenda get away, and he wasn't going to make the same mistake twice.

BOOOP! BOOOP! BOOOP! sounded the theft detector.

"Hey, you!" the clerk shouted.

Eddie was waiting just outside, wearing a casual grin. "I put a few electronic goodies in your backpack," he said. "I think we'd better run."

"Stop! Thief! Police!" the clerk yelled.

Cole looked over his shoulder . . . and took off down the street.

"Not *that* way!" Eddie called out. "Over here!"

Eddie was heading for the edge of a wooded

area. Cole followed him through the trees, tripping on roots and catching branches in the face.

"Faster!" Eddie seemed to glide easily over the terrain, scrambling down an embankment. "I know you can do it!"

Cole breathed heavily, weighed down by his pack. The embankment was steep. Cole rolled down, grasping at branches that slipped out of his hands.

He ended up in the middle of a narrow road at the bottom.

A bicycle sped around the curve, swerving as it braked. Cole leaped to the shoulder of the road, barely missing a collision.

On the other side of the road, Eddie was laughing his head off.

"It's not funny!" Cole shouted, getting out of the bicyclist's way. "You could've killed me!"

"I didn't make you run like that," Eddie said. "You should have seen the look on your face!"

Cole brushed himself off and started back in the direction of the electronics store. "I was trying to tell you something! Something you'd want to know. About your *girlfriend*. But I guess you don't need to know the details."

"Hey!" Eddie called after him. "Where are you going?"

"Back to the store. To return the stuff you made me steal."

Eddie ran in front of him. "Whoa — take it easy for second. I only did that because I knew you could take it. You're a lot like me, kid. We're both rebels. I'll bet you don't know the trouble you could be."

Cole stopped for second. This was definitely the first time anyone had ever called him a *rebel*. Eddie was the first person to see him at all that way.

"You're just making fun of me," Cole said quietly.

"Not at all! You've got guts. More than most people twice your age. Don't you realize that? Not many people would've chased me like that. They would've just given up. But you don't give up, do you?"

Cole didn't know what to say. Sure, his mom thought he was brave — but even when she was saying he was brave, she was still thinking he needed her protection. The kids at school would *never* have thought of him as someone with guts. Right now even his best friend was probably thinking he was a wimp for letting Brenda get away.

But Eddie didn't see him that way.

Cole liked that. He liked to believe that he wasn't the kind of kid who gave up.

"I saw a photo in Brenda's house of you and Brenda," Cole said, not letting up now.

"I'm sure it was an old picture," Eddie replied.

"No, it wasn't. You wrote the date on the back. And you gave her a mix tape with some songs on it that are still on the radio. I saw it in the warehouse."

"She had it with her?"

"Yeah. She said it was her favorite."

Eddie took a deep breath.

Cole had gotten through to him.

"Why are you doing this?" Eddie asked. "I mean, why do you care?"

"At first it was because Ted is my friend's brother. But I'm doing it for Brenda and her family, too."

Eddie sat down on the ground. "I might know where they are," he said.

"Where?"

"They're with Spider."

This struck the wrong note with Cole. "You tried that one already," he said.

"Yeah, and Spider blew you off. But he's the gate-keeper. He's the one you have to go through."

"And then what happens?"

Eddie shook his head. "I don't know. Honestly. I only know the part up to Spider. After that — nothing. But if you get to him, you'll get to the runaways."

"But I asked him already . . ." Cole started. But as soon as he said it, he knew what Eddie's answer would be:

Asking isn't enough.

"With a guy like Spider, you have to get him on your side first," Eddie said. "I was never able to do that. But you might. You don't look dangerous. But you and I know the truth. You're stronger than that."

Am I really? Cole thought.

"How am I supposed to get through to him?" he asked.

For the first time since Cole had met him, Eddie's look was totally serious.

"Any way you can," he said. "But you'll only have one chance."

FIFTEEN

Cole knew where he had to go.

Back to Grendel's.

First he tried calling Detective Brown with the cell phone in his pocket. Jason had forgotten to reclaim it when he left Cole at the multiplex. But the detective was out and couldn't be reached. Since Cole knew that Detective Brown would trust him, he left him a voicemail telling him about what Brenda and Eddie had said.

He hoped no one else would hear it.

He also left the number of the cell phone. He figured since he was using it to help find the runaways, Jason's mom wouldn't mind.

He hoped Detective Brown would call him soon.

But in the meantime, he had to keep trying.

Grendel's was crowded as usual. Eddie was there, but he stayed back, laying low.

It was up to Cole now.

He knew it would be foolish to go straight to the back room and demand that Spider listen to him again. There had to be another way to get through.

But how?

Cole decided to wait by the Coke machine, right outside the black curtain. He made sure it didn't look like he was too eager to go in. Instead he was just hanging out. Calmly.

Merv and his posse walked by, shooting Cole nasty looks. But they didn't do anything. Apparently, Devon's warning still held.

Devon also saw Cole, but didn't say a word. Maybe he didn't even recognize him. After all, they'd only met once.

Cole tried to pay attention to his surroundings. A few people went inside the black curtain, and a few people came out from behind. He didn't recognize any of them.

But one of them must have recognized him. About forty minutes after Cole had first arrived, Spider came out from behind the curtain and headed right for him.

Stay calm, Cole told himself. *Don't give up.*

"You're back," Spider said flatly. "I thought I told you to go."

Cole stayed silent.

Spider seemed to admire that. "Don't you have somewhere to be?" he asked.

"No." Cole looked for Eddie, for support, but couldn't see him anywhere.

"Have you run away?"

Cole didn't know why, but he found himself saying, "Yes."

Spider arched an eyebrow under his shaved head. "Really? Why?"

"My dad left. I want to leave, too." Cole felt strange mixing a truth and a lie like this, but he could tell it caused Spider to like him more.

Still, Spider wasn't going to make it easy.

"So you're running away," he snarled. "What do you want — a permission slip?"

"No. I want you take me to the place where the others went."

Spider shook his head. "I don't know what you're talking about."

Don't give up.

"Yes, you do. Ted told me."

"Did he? I guess he was lying to you, kid."

Cole knew he was losing. He had one last shot.

"Plus," he lied, "I know where Brenda is."

This startled Spider — Cole could tell.

He could sense Spider teetering. So he added, "I'm sure Thorn would want to know where she is."

That did it.

"Come with me," Spider said. Then he pushed back the black curtain and led Cole inside.

SIXTEEN

They walked through the room Cole had been in before. It was empty now. There was a door in the back that Cole hadn't noticed in the darkness. They went through that, and then headed down a twisted route of stairs. Finally, they ended up in a dark tunnel, somewhere underneath the building.

"Watch your head," Spider said. His voice echoed off the walls. The thin beam of his flashlight glided over the decayed tiles, crumbling and stained.

What am I doing? Cole thought, touching the phone in his pocket. *Maybe Eddie was wrong. Maybe everyone else is right.*

Maybe I really am *a wimp.*

And a wimp shouldn't be doing this.

Cole felt something thick and pulsating beneath

115

his feet. He jumped back but didn't see anything move away.

I am doing this for Jason.

I am doing this for Brenda's family.

I am doing this for all the other people left behind.

Spider was walking ahead quickly, his wet footsteps mixing with the steady drip-drip-drip of unidentified fluids from the ceiling.

They kept going downward. They were well under the city by now.

The smell was dank and rancid — almost unbearable.

Spider saw Cole scrunching up his face.

"You get used to it," he said. Then he stopped short.

An animal the size of a small cat came splashing toward them, then veered away.

Spider trained his flashlight on the creature.

A rat.

Cole nearly hit the ceiling.

"Stay away from those," Spider said.

"Thanks," Cole replied.

The rat leaped in the air and skittered into a hole.

"People *like* coming here?" Cole asked.

"It's better when you get inside," Spider explained.

"Inside?"

Spider shone his light on a small, battered metal door. Above it was a faded sign that read FALLOUT SHELTER.

"Here we are."

Cole hesitated. He didn't know what was on the other side of the door.

He wasn't sure he wanted to know.

Spider was getting impatient. "C'mon. Just open it. There's no going back now."

Cole felt a chill come over him. He turned away from Spider and saw Mr. Merchant standing a few feet away, not saying a word.

Don't give up.

Cole was strangely reassured by the dead man's presence.

He was pretty sure that this time Mr. Merchant wouldn't run away.

Cole tried to look confident. He grabbed hold of the knob and pulled.

The door swung open with a loud creak.

Inside was an enormous, vaulted room, its graffiti-covered walls bathed in the flickering blue light of three TV sets. A pattern of bare lightbulbs provided the only other illumination, which wasn't much.

The din of laughter and conversation spilled out into the tunnel. Cole could feel the beat of a stereo — the dark musical undertone to an underground world. Over a dozen high-school-age kids milled around inside, some talking, some watching TV. On the floor, a few people sprawled in sleeping bags and under blankets. At the back of the room, Cole could make out more doors.

"Welcome to the underground," Spider said proudly.

From all corners, eyes stared at Cole.

"But — I thought there were only seven runaways," Cole said.

"Reported," Spider corrected. "In the Philly area. Kids from all over hear about this place. We ought to charge admission. But Thorn's not like that."

Cole wondered which one of these people was Thorn.

"I don't know how he found these shelters," Spider continued, "but I'm glad he did. I think they were supposed to save all the government dudes in case of nuclear bombs or whatever. Anyway, after a while it got too expensive to keep up, so they sealed it off. Or at least they thought they sealed it off."

"How do you get out?" Cole asked.

Spider looked at him defensively. "You don't need to," he said. "Everything you need is here. Thorn makes sure of that."

Cole looked at the faces that were looking at him. Some of them seemed happy.

Some of them did not.

One of them made Cole stop cold.

There, coming from the back of the room, was Ted Black.

SEVENTEEN

Spider saw him, too.

"Hey, Ted," he called out. "I brought a friend of yours underground."

Uh-oh. Cole hadn't planned on this. He had lied to Spider and said that Ted told him about the place. But Ted didn't know that — he might not even remember that Cole was Jason's friend. If he said he'd told Cole anything, they might all be in big trouble. Especially Cole.

Cole held his breath as Ted came closer, looking at him curiously. He searched for any flicker of recognition. He tried to send a signal through his eyes —

Pretend that you know me.

Don't let Spider know that you don't.

"What are you doing here?" Ted finally asked. He didn't sound pleased — but at least he sounded like he knew Cole.

"You see what kind of influence you have?" Spider joked to Ted. "This guy wanted to join you. Plus, he has news for Thorn. I'm going to go get him."

Ted stared at Cole for a moment after Spider left through one of the far doors. Then he pulled him aside, into a small, dingy room filled with cereal boxes, day-old donuts, and quickly rotting fruit. With a start, Cole realized that this was the kitchen.

"You're Jason's friend, right?" Ted said quietly, careful not to be overheard.

Cole nodded.

"You shouldn't be here. You're way too young."

"I came to find you," Cole explained. "We have to go."

Ted shook his head. "No — *you* should go. My place is here."

Cole looked around the dark, dank room. "Why?" he asked.

"Because I can't go home. This is my home now. I can't leave."

Cole was surprised. He hadn't thought this would happen. He figured all he had to do was find Ted — and then they'd both head back.

But Ted was refusing to go.

"They're all worried about you," Cole said, trying to keep his voice low even though his mind wanted to scream. "Jason can't sleep at night because he's so worried about finding you. Your mom cries all the time. You dad has driven down every street in Philadelphia looking for you. Kent and your other friends have hung up posters everywhere. The police are searching for you nonstop. Your family even went on TV to ask you to come back. You might not know that down here, but it's true."

"You don't understand what it was like," Ted argued, a little less forcefully than before.

"Maybe not," Cole agreed, "But *you* don't understand what it's like *now*." He pulled Mrs. Black's cell phone from his pocket. "Just call them, Ted. Call them right now. You'll see how much they miss you."

"Put that away!" Ted whispered sharply.

"No," Cole said, standing his ground, thinking of Jason and his mom and his dad at home, knowing this was the only call that would make them okay again. "Call them."

Ted stared at the phone for a moment. Then he took it from Cole and, turning his back to the doorway, started to dial. Cole started to relax a moment — then Ted cursed.

"What?" Cole asked.

Ted showed him the phone.

No service, the display read.

They were too far underground to get a signal.

Without warning, a tattooed arm reached over Ted's shoulder and snatched the phone away.

"Sorry, against house rules," a gruff, gravely voice announced.

Cole looked up as Ted spun around to face a giant of a man. He was maybe six-foot-four, his face boney and broad, his hair dyed jet black. He stuffed the phone into the pocket of a jean jacket that was emblazoned with the grotesque insect–rat symbol. His tone of voice made it clear that he expected to be listened to.

Spider appeared at the man's side, blocking the doorway.

"This is the kid, Thorn," he said, pointing at Cole.

But Thorn wasn't through with Ted yet. He grabbed him by the throat and squeezed.

"No phones, understand?" he growled. Then he threw Ted to the floor.

Cole leaned over to him.

"Are you okay?" he asked.

"Fine," Ted grunted.

Cole helped him to his feet. Ted brushed off the cereal flakes and fruit peels that stuck to his clothes.

"So I hear you have some information for me," Thorn said, turning his rough eye on Cole.

Cole nodded quietly and put his hands behind his back, so Thorn wouldn't see them shaking.

"You know where Brenda is?"

"Yes."

"Where is she, then?"

Cole was sure Brenda would never go back to the warehouse, so he said, "At an old meat factory," and gave the address.

Thorn shook his head slowly, so Cole would know he'd been caught in a lie. "Wrong," he said, stepping back from the doorway. "She's right here."

For the first time since Thorn had appeared, Cole could see into the main room.

And there was Brenda, arms held by two angry-looking men.

Trapped.

EIGHTEEN

After Brenda had stopped resisting, the two guys let her go.

"Walk around all you want," Thorn taunted. "You're not going to leave and betray us again."

"You don't control me," Brenda said defiantly. Everyone in the room was paying attention now.

"This isn't about control," Thorn said gently, turning to the rest of the room. "Is it?"

A chorus of murmured "no's" answered him.

"It's about safety," Thorn continued. "It's about democracy. No one is better than anyone else here. If they can stay, so can you. Don't forget — if one of us lets out the word, it's over for everyone else. And we don't want that to happen."

"I didn't tell anyone," Brenda said.

"I know. But that doesn't mean you won't in the future. So you stay here."

"What about Eddie?" Brenda adked. "Is he a part of this? He's here, isn't he?"

Thorn smirked and shrugged — no answer.

Everyone steered clear of Brenda, even after Thorn left the room. Cole was the first person to go over to her. After a moment's hesitation, Ted followed. Mr. Merchant hung in the background, still silent. Watching.

"Are you okay?" Ted asked Brenda.

"No," she replied frankly, "I'm not at all okay. I'm back here."

Ted shook his head. "It's not that bad, Bren. You really shouldn't have left."

Brenda looked at Ted like he was an alien. "You should hear yourself, Ted. You're as bad as the rest of them. They kidnapped me and dragged me back here — do you understand that? *I don't want to be here.*"

"They were only worried about everyone else," Ted said. "They were worried you'd tell everyone where we are."

"Do you honestly believe that, Ted?" Brenda raised her voice, knowing she was being overheard. "Do *any of you* believe that? Here are the facts. Thorn is a criminal. A thug. He is running from the law. He invented this hideaway and let other run-aways come here. He's *using you.* He says it's a democracy, but that's a total lie. Freedom means being able to leave whenever you want to leave. But can you?"

"We don't *want* to leave," one kid shouted.

Brenda turned back to Ted. "Look at you," she said to him. "Are you really happy here? Do you really feel free?"

Ted stepped back abruptly.

"That's none of your business, Bren." He turned to look at Cole. "Or yours. Just leave me alone. Both of you. I need to think."

He headed back across the room. Cole went to follow, but Brenda stopped him.

"If he says he wants to be left alone, then he wants to be left alone," she said. "He has to figure it out on his own."

Cole wasn't sure they had that much time.

Brenda walked back into a small alcove where a thin mat covered part of the cement floor. Cole watched as she picked up the mat and let it drop. A photo was hidden underneath. Somebody else's.

"This used to be my space," she said listlessly. "I guess they gave it to someone new." Pausing, she studied Cole for a moment.

"So who are you, really?" she asked. "If you're

not working for Thorn, then what are you doing here?"

"I was looking for you. And Ted. That's all."

He could feel Mr. Merchant in the room. There were so many things Cole couldn't say.

"I thought about going home," Brenda said, her toughness crumbling. "I should've when I had a chance. But I was sure that Thorn would find me there. He'd made so many threats . . . I couldn't risk one of them coming true."

"I need to talk to you —" Cole began.

But Brenda cut him off. "I have nothing to say to you. I have nothing to say to anyone. Nobody cares about me, so I don't care about them. Maybe you should leave me alone, too."

"But people do care," Cole said. "Your mom, your brother, your dad —"

Brenda laughed. "Not my dad."

If you only knew . . .

Wordlessly, Eddie entered the room. He smiled sadly at Brenda — but she didn't return it. Instead, she shivered and turned away, fighting back tears. "Go away," she said softly.

"I can't when you're like this. I know I have a lot of explaining to do. I'm sorry you're back here." Eddie shook his head sadly and turned to Cole. "She believes this stuff, Cole. She believes that nobody cares about her. I always tell her how great she is, smart and strong and beautiful and talented — she used to listen to me, too. But then she just stopped. It's like talking to a tree."

"Knock it off!" Brenda said. "And stop looking at me like that."

Eddie gestured exaggeratedly to Cole, as if to say *Talk to her.*

"They care about you," Cole said. "Deep in your heart, you know they do."

Brenda's shoulders sagged. She exhaled hard, her voice distant. "Eddie cared. He cared a lot. But now look what's happened. I met him after Dad left, and he really helped take away some of the sting. He was older than me — I guess I thought that meant he knew how to deal more. He didn't have it so good himself. His mom died when he was a baby and his dad was a serious wacko. When Eddie was four, his dad would leave him at home for days at a time, totally alone."

Eddie nodded. "I had to make my own meals, and I didn't know how to use any of the appliances. I put a frozen pizza in the oven without taking it out of the box first. I nearly set the house on fire."

"After that he went to live with his aunt Margie," Brenda continued. "Well, she *hated* kids, especially one that her brother-in-law was too lazy to take care of. So when he was old enough, he told her good-bye. He got a place of his own and didn't leave her an address. I met him around then. He had no family left."

"Nobody to ever report me missing," Eddie added.

"He also didn't have much money, so he soon lost the place where he was living. We decided to be together anyway. We met Spider and he told us about this place. He made it sound like one nonstop party, anything goes — but he wasn't going to tell us where it was until we committed ourselves. Well, we decided to do it. He just had one last thing to do — some guy was going to pay him to drive a car to Cleveland. We needed the money, so he said okay."

"It was supposed to take two days," Eddie said, holding his forehead. "It sounded like it would be really easy."

Brenda turned and looked directly at Cole, her eyes rimmed red. "Eddie never came back. That was the last time I saw him. I thought maybe he'd be here. But he's not, is he?"

NINETEEN

Brenda was sobbing now, all of her toughness drained away.

Eddie looked at her sadly. "I was in such a hurry. I wanted to get back so we could start our life. I didn't sleep much the night before, and I was speeding really bad. It was late at night and the highway was empty. I guess I nodded off a little bit behind the wheel. Because when I woke up, everything was different. The car was trashed and I couldn't get back to Brenda on time. When I finally made it to Philadelphia, she had already gone underground."

He doesn't realize, Cole thought.

He died in that car crash.

He's dead now.

"I'm so cold," Brenda whispered, shaking.

"Here, have my coat," Eddie offered. He unzipped his jacket and took it off.

Cole had to turn away. In one glance, he saw enough.

Eddie had a grotesquely flattened torso under the bulky coat. Four ribs protruded from a bloody tear in his side.

"It's okay," Cole told him.

Eddie put the jacket back on and shrugged. He looked at Brenda with a longing that was at the same time hopeless yet genuine.

He needs me to help her, Cole thought. *And then he can move on.*

Just like her dad.

"Can you find a way out?" Cole asked Mr. Merchant.

"I'm sure they blocked the one I took last time," Brenda answered, looking up at Cole from her tears.

"I know one," Eddie said. "I found a back way. Let's go."

Eddie began walking to the back of the room, where an open archway led into a narrow, dark corridor.

"Brenda —?" Cole began

"Y — yes."

"We have to go."

He looked for Eddie in the dark.

"Cole, you're scaring me. What are you staring at?"

Eddie, having disappeared, now returned and poked his head in the alcove. "Hurry!" he cried.

"I think I know a way," Cole told Brenda. "Follow me . . . before Thorn comes back."

It was easy for Eddie to negotiate the escape route. He was dead.

But for Cole and Brenda, it was another story.

The hallway was pitch-black. Not one light. The floor was so caked with grime that it stuck to Cole's shoes in clumps.

His heart beat rapidly. He knew Thorn would go after them as soon as he realized they were gone.

How long would that be?

"Where are we going?" Brenda demanded.

"Sssshhhh," Cole said, listening for Eddie's footsteps.

When Eddie veered right, Cole followed.

He smacked his head on the wall.

"Ow!" Cole cried out. "You could have warned me!"

"How could I warn you?" Brenda hissed. "I'm behind you!"

Pulling Brenda down with him, Cole crawled through a rough, pitted cylinder that must have been a working pipe of some sort.

"There are tubes down here," Eddie said. "A whole network to transport food and oxygen and water and people to the fallout shelters, in case of Armadillon."

"Armageddon," Cole corrected him.

"What?" Brenda said.

"Never mind."

"The construction crew must have thought they sealed them all off," Eddie went on. "But they didn't."

Cole felt his wrist pulled forward. He tumbled through a hole in the pipe and landed hard on a stone floor.

Brenda screamed as she tumbled after him.

"Cole, this is ridiculous!" she said. "I'm heading back. At least I know I won't get killed back there."

"No!" Eddie exclaimed.

"No!" Cole echoed. "Look, we can stand up here. We're getting closer."

"Closer to *what*?" Brenda asked.

Cole didn't know.

"This is the secondary conduit," Eddie explained, walking ahead. "It leads to the rest of the city."

Cole could see a small circle of dim light ahead, suspended in midair. He saw Eddie pass in front of it briefly.

Cole stepped forward cautiously and reached out. The hole was set in what felt like a thick metal wall.

Another dead end.

"What do we do now?" Cole whispered to Eddie.

"I was about to ask you the same question!" Brenda snapped.

"Pull," Eddie said.

Cole reached his hand into the hole, grabbed onto the metal, and yanked it toward him.

He wasn't strong enough to do it on his own.

"Give me a hand!" he yelled to Brenda. "Let's pull this thing toward us."

"You can do it, Cole," Eddie said, standing aside. "I know you can."

"This hole?" Brenda asked, sliding next to Cole and squeezing her hand next to his. They both held tight and leaned back with all their weight.

Slowly, with a loud noise, the metal swung inward. On a hinge.

They worked hard, pulling the door open wide enough to squeeze through.

"Cole, you did it!" Brenda exclaimed. "You're a genius."

She kissed him impulsively on the cheek. Cole felt himself blushing.

"Go on," Eddie urged. "Let's get out of here and find help!"

Cole ran out the crack in the door. He took a few steps, then lost his footing and fell.

A stab of pain ran up his leg from the place where he'd caught his ankle. His face was in gravel, his head against a steel bar.

The ground began to shake. A gust of air whooshed overhead and a rumbling noise mixed with the noise of a loud horn.

A subway train was coming.

"Cole, get up!" Brenda shouted. *"Get up!"*

Cole jumped to his feet. He clasped his hands to form a boost for Brenda and pushed her up to the platform.

"Grab my arm!" she said. "Now!"

Cole reached out for her — and his ankle buckled.

He fell back onto the track bed, just missing the electrified third rail.

The train's brakes screeched, the headlights almost upon him. People yelled on the platform. Cole felt the sparks of the wheels against the track.

One last pull.

"Come on, *be strong*," Eddie whispered to him.

Cole closed his eyes and felt his leg lift up.

Brenda grabbed him and pulled.

The next thing he knew, he was sprawled on the platform. The train barreled into the station. Cole turned, looking back to the tracks.

Eddie was still there. He nodded to Cole and mouthed the words *I love you* to Brenda as the train passed over him.

Cole flinched. He had to remind himself that Eddie was already dead.

Part of him had the urge to wait until the train pulled out of the station. Just to be sure.

But Cole knew Eddie would be gone. He had no reason to stay any more.

He'd brought Brenda back.

A crowd was now huddled around the two of them, everyone screaming and asking questions.

Cole stood and tested his ankle. He could walk.

"Come on," he said, taking Brenda's hand. "We're calling the police."

TWENTY

Within a half hour, Cole was back at Grendel's — this time with Detective Brown and a large part of the Philadelphia police department.

Brenda was back with her mom and her brother. They had come to the subway station as soon as Brenda had called. The three of them held one another like they'd never let go.

Mr. Merchant stood to the side, watching.

Now Cole had to lead Detective Brown to the door that would take them underground.

"After that, you stay back," the detective made clear.

The cop cars swarmed around the arcade entrance. Detective Brown barged his way inside, with Cole in tow.

"Police!" another officer yelled, holding out his badge.

"It's a raid!" someone yelled.

People began to fight to reach the exits. Some of the more hardcore players stuck to their machines, oblivious.

Detective Brown was veering toward the Coke machine.

"Behind the curtain!" Cole shouted.

The black drape parted, and Spider emerged. He took one look at the scene and started to run away.

Detective Brown lunged and pinned Spider to the wall.

"I believe you're about to give me an underground tour," the cop said.

Spider saw Cole and fixed him with a murderous glance.

"You!" he shouted.

Detective Brown grabbed his chin and faced him straight again, so that he was forced to look in the detective's eyes.

"Leave him out of it," he said sharply. "This is between you, me, and the hundred or so other police officers surrounding the building."

Spider gave in then. Cole could see it. He went from a fighting pose to a resigned defeat.

He would show Detective Brown the way.

Hopefully it wouldn't be too late.

There was no telling what Thorn would do.

The minutes seemed like hours as Cole waited for Detective Brown to come back out from the underground. At first, it was just him and the police, who were busy sorting out the kids from Grendel's and closing the place down. Then the families started to come; they'd been told what was happening, and they rushed to the arcade to see their children again. Jason was there with his mom and his dad. Brenda came with her mom and her brother. Lynn pushed her way through the police barricade to be with Cole. She didn't ask him any questions about what he'd done. They'd have to find a way to talk about it later.

As they waited, Jason came over.

"I'm sorry I was mad at you," he said to Cole.

"No problem," Cole answered. And it really wasn't, not anymore.

There was sudden activity on the police radio. Cole could hear Detective Brown's voice:

"We've got 'em — everybody's okay!"

A cheer went out in the crowd. Parents cried out of relief.

Then came more waiting . . . until finally the runaways appeared.

Cole anxiously watched their faces. There were two guys he'd seen inside. One girl.

And then Ted.

For a moment, Cole was worried. What if Ted still didn't want to go back? What if he tried to run away again?

Ted's eyes scanned the crowd, dazed. Then he saw his family and ran . . . right into their arms.

Mr. and Mrs. Black clutched each other tight as Jason enfolded himself around his brother.

"Ted!" he cried, as if couldn't believe it.

Soon they were all hugging, crying.

They were a family again.

Later on, Jason and Ted would come over and thank Cole. Later on, Detective Brown would emerge with Thorn in a pair of handcuffs. Later on — later that night — Cole would tell Mr. Merchant to apologize to his family while they slept, so that they might be able to hear him, and he could move on. Later on, Brenda would find out the truth about Eddie, and that he hadn't meant to leave her.

But right now, none of those things were on Cole's mind. Instead, he watched the reunions and thought about what they meant. He saw how happy everyone was — there were no questions, no arguments, no regrets. Just the joy of being together. Just the happiness of being whole.

Deep in his heart, Cole still wanted a reunion of his own. Just one last moment of total happiness with his mom and his dad before reality hit.

Lynn put her hands on Cole's shoulders and squeezed.

"I'm so proud of you," she said.

Cole reached up and touched her hands. Maybe Eddie was right — maybe he was a little bit of a rebel. Maybe he was stronger than he'd first believed. He didn't get that from his father, who'd run away. He got that from his mother, who'd stayed. If he was at all brave, it was because he had had a good role model.

They would never need to have a reunion.

They would always have each other.